STAR WARS®

JEDI APPRENTICE

The Uncertain Path

Jude Watson

LUCAS BOOKS

SCHOLASTIC INC.

New York Toronto London Auckland Sydney
Mexico City New Delhi Hong Kong

ISBN 0-590-51969-7

12 11 10 9 8 7 6 5 4 3 2 1   0 1 2 3 4 5 6/0

Printed in the U.S.A.
First Scholastic printing, February 2000

Obi-Wan Kenobi paced between rows of tombs in a tunnel below the city of Zehava. Overhead, a battle raged. The noise of the explosions was muffled. But every time Obi-Wan heard the faint *thump* of a proton torpedo, he had to stop himself from wincing. His imagination supplied the damage the explosive device had inflicted. The enemy had starfighters, and the ground forces of the Young were being bombarded.

Around him, the shapes of other tombs loomed in the murky darkness. The Young had made their headquarters in the tunnels below the city. They had chosen the vaulted space of an ancient mausoleum as central headquarters.

"Obi-Wan, sit down," his friend Cerasi called. "You're making me dizzy."

In moments of crisis, Cerasi was always calm. Nield, a tall slender boy with dark eyes, was more serious. Obi-Wan could see the strain on their faces. He could not remember the last time any of them had eaten or slept. They had been fighting aboveground for fourteen days. Now they waited for the news that seemed long in coming.

The three had led the Young on a quest to bring peace to the planet of Melida/Daan. Their war with the Elders was yet another war in the bloody history of Melida/Daan. The planet had been torn by conflict for centuries, as the two tribes, Melida and Daan, struggled for control. It was the Young who had finally called for peace. The Elders had refused, and now the children of Melida/Daan were battling to save their planet.

Obi-Wan had never believed in a cause more. He had forsaken his Jedi training because of it. After struggling to become Padawan to the great Jedi Knight Qui-Gon Jinn, he had turned his back on him to battle for peace on a strange planet.

Sometimes, he could not believe that he'd made the decision. Then he would look at his friends and remember why he had done so. He had never felt as close to anyone as he did to Nield and Cerasi.

Cerasi's crystal green eyes gleamed in a face streaked with dirt and sweat. She patted a space on top of the tomb where she sat with

Nield. "I'm sure Mawat will clear the tunnel to the spaceport any moment now," she assured Obi-Wan.

"He has to," Obi-Wan said worriedly as he took his place between them. "We have to strike when the starfighters are being refueled. It's our only hope."

Obi-Wan had been the one to notice that the fleet of starfighters all attacked in the same wave. Most of the advanced weaponry on Melida/Daan had to be constantly retooled and refitted. The people had been fighting so long that equipment was worn out. The aging starfighters had to be refueled and checked more frequently. And the Elders' mistake was that they were refueling their entire fleet *at the same time.*

Which meant they were vulnerable.

Obi-Wan's plan was to invade the spaceport with a small team during the refueling process. While one member of the team disabled the power converters on the starfighters, the others would serve as lookouts. If a battle started, the first objective was to distract the guards.

It was risky, but if they were successful, victory would be assured. Recently, the Middle Generation had offered their support to the Young. They would form an alliance, but only if victory was in sight. If the Young gained the support of the few who remained of the Middle Generation, the Elders would be outnumbered.

Mawat, the leader of the Scavenger Young, was now working to expand a small side tunnel into the spaceport's power shaft. From there they would be able to enter the port through a grate in the floor.

"All we need is timing and luck," Cerasi said.

Obi-Wan grinned. "Who, us? We don't need luck."

"Everybody needs luck," Nield shot back.

"Not us."

They held out their palms toward each other, their hands as close as they could without touching. The gesture was a ritual they'd developed through the many battles over the past weeks.

Suddenly, a small, slender girl rushed into the vault. "Mawat says we're clear."

"Thanks, Roenni," Obi-Wan said, springing to his feet. "Are you ready?"

She nodded and held up a pair of fusioncutters. "I'm ready."

He hated to involve Roenni. She was younger and unused to battle, but her father had been a starfighter mechanic. She'd grown up around every kind of air transport available. She knew how to use a fusioncutter, and how to disable a power converter. Obi-Wan was counting on the fact that she was small and agile. She could slip into the starfighter through the cargo hold below. With any luck, she could do it without being seen.

Obi-Wan, Nield, Cerasi, and Roenni hurried through the tunnels. When they got to the new tunnel immediately beneath the spaceport, they moved more carefully. They were now directly below the guards.

Mawat came toward them. His lean face was completely covered in dirt and muck. His clothes were filthy.

"Took longer because we had to work so quietly," he murmured to them. "But, hey, you'll come up right behind the fueling tanks. Three of the starfighters are, *bang,* lined up next to them. Two are close to the entrance. There are two utility droids and six guards. At least, *blast,* they won't be expecting you to come from below."

Remember, Padawan, when you are outnumbered, surprise is your best ally.

Qui-Gon's calm voice entered Obi-Wan's mind, twining through his apprehension like a cool river. He felt a pang. He had never carried off an operation like this without his Master by his side.

Obi-Wan reached out to the Force. He would need it in this battle. But the Force slipped away from him like an unseen sea creature that brushed against him and then moved on. He could not reach it or summon it. He could only imagine its great power.

The Force had left him.

Leave you, the Force cannot. Constant, it is. If find it you cannot, look inside, not out, you must.

Yes, Yoda, Obi-Wan thought. *Look inside, I should. But how can I when I'm in the middle of a war?*

"Obi-Wan?" Cerasi touched his shoulder. "It's time."

Obi-Wan moved the grate aside carefully. He boosted Roenni up and then followed. Cerasi swung herself out with her usual agility. Nield clambered up a little clumsily, but without making a noise.

They crouched behind the fueling tanks. The utility droids, working busily to refuel the starfighters, didn't notice them. Nor did the guards, who stood at the entrance of the spaceport, their backs to the grate. Obi-Wan nodded toward the first starfighter, and Roenni streaked across to climb inside through the cargo hold.

There were only five starfighters. Three were parked side by side. With luck, Roenni could disable them quickly and quietly. The trick would be to get to the last two, which were parked closer to the entrance ... and the guards.

Cerasi, Nield, and Obi-Wan watched anxiously, their weapons at the ready, as Roenni ran from one starfighter to another. After the third, she poked her head out and gestured to the group. *What now?*

Obi-Wan leaned close to Cerasi and Nield. "I'll go with Roenni," he whispered. He did not want to send the girl across the expanse alone. "Hopefully, the guards won't turn around. You cover us."

His friends nodded. Obi-Wan moved quietly past the three starfighters, keeping away from the utility droids. He reached Roenni's side. The girl's dark eyes were fearful as she looked at the space they would need to cross. He squeezed her shoulder for reassurance, and she nodded with more confidence. They took off across the empty space, running quickly and silently.

They might have made it if a utility droid hadn't knocked into an empty fuel barrel. It rolled noisily across the floor and came to rest a few centimeters from their feet. One of the guards turned. Obi-Wan saw the surprise on his face as he registered the two invaders.

"Hey!" the guard called.

In the split second it took for the guard to fully recognize the threat, Obi-Wan was already moving. He gave Roenni a push toward the starfighters, then ran toward a stack of dura-steel cargo boxes. He made an enormous leap and landed on top of them, then used the momentum to hurl himself at the guard. As blaster fire erupted around his head, he fervently wished he had his lightsaber. He had given it to Qui-Gon to take back to the Temple. Only the Jedi could carry lightsabers.

He could see the guard's mouth drop in surprise as Obi-Wan hurtled toward him, feet first. He knocked him down, then grabbed his blaster.

The second guard turned just in time to see the first go down. Obi-Wan was already whirling, coming at the guard with a kick to the chin. The guard fell, cracking his head against the stone floor. His blaster rifle skidded away, and Obi-Wan jumped back toward Nield. Nield and Cerasi had already begun moving forward, firing at the guards.

The four remaining guards scattered. They were all wearing plastoid armor, but no one took chances with blaster fire. They fired as they ran, and Obi-Wan leaped back around the boxes for cover. Nield and Cerasi joined him a split second later.

"They've probably called for help on their

comlinks," Cerasi said grimly as she took aim at the guards, who were crouching behind a pile of disabled floaters. She fired rapidly over one guard's head as he tried to take a clear shot.

Obi-Wan saw Roenni frantically signal from the starfighter. "We need to cover Roenni," he told the others. "Keep firing."

They kept up a rapid stream of blaster fire. Roenni scooted under the belly of one starfighter and leaped into the next.

"Last one," Obi-Wan said.

Two guards suddenly split off from the others and dashed to either side of the spaceport, ducking behind pillars for cover.

"They're trying to get behind us!" Obi-Wan alerted Cerasi and Nield. Then he ran to the other end of the cargo boxes, keeping under cover. Roenni hadn't seen the guards' maneuver. She leaped down from the last starfighter at the same instant that the guard behind the pillar stepped out to fire. Obi-Wan saw him catch sight of the young girl, whirl, and aim.

Desperately, Obi-Wan reached out for the Force. This time, he felt it surge around him. He put out his hand, and the blaster flew from the surprised guard's hand. The blaster fire went awry and pinged harmlessly into the wall.

Roenni stood, paralyzed with fear. Obi-Wan

dashed to her side while Cerasi and Nield kept up a barrage at the guards. Panic swirled in Roenni's eyes as she gazed at Obi-Wan.

"I'm right here." Obi-Wan locked eyes with her, hoping to drive away the fear. "I won't let anything happen to you."

Roenni's brown eyes cleared. Trust drove out fear. But Cerasi and Nield couldn't keep the guards down forever. They were exposed. Obi-Wan spotted the empty fuel drum the droid had knocked over. He reached out with the Force. Nothing.

Never gone. Always there, it is.

Obi-Wan groaned. *You think so, Yoda? Not for me!*

Blaster fire ripped into the fuselage of the starfighter over his head. Obi-Wan pushed Roenni down. Keeping his body bent over hers, he ran, hunched over, to the barrel. Not the greatest protection, but it would have to do.

"We're going to have to crawl," he told Roenni. "Keep yourself behind the barrel."

Roenni crawled in front of him as he pushed the barrel steadily toward Nield and Cerasi. Blaster fire pinged off the metal. Obi-Wan could feel Roenni shaking. When they reached the pile of cargo boxes, she slid behind them with relief.

Obi-Wan rolled the huge barrel toward the

front guard. It smashed into his knees, and he fell backward into the guard behind him. They teetered into the line of fire of the other guards.

The four friends took advantage of the moment and ran, firing as they went. They reached the safety of the fuel tanks. Cerasi was the most nimble of them all. She hustled Roenni down, then followed. With a last blast, Nield jumped down. Obi-Wan slid through the opening, then threw out a timed explosive device.

"Run!" he yelled.

They all scrambled to safety — and then the tank exploded, taking most of the hangar with it.

"That should keep them busy," he told the others.

Nield raised Mawat on the comlink. "It's done," he said. "The Elders have no starfighters anymore. You can contact the Middle Generation."

Mawat's voice crackled over the comlink. Though the transmission was faint, they could hear his glee.

"I think we just won the war!" he crowed.

CHAPTER 2

The lightsaber came down, missing him by millimeters. Qui-Gon jumped away, surprised. The blow came from nowhere. He hadn't been paying attention.

He whirled, raising his own lightsaber in defense. His opponent parried, then twisted away to come at him from his left. Their lightsabers tangled, buzzing. Suddenly, his opponent shifted his feet and moved right. Qui-Gon hadn't expected the move, and his dodge was ill-timed. The lightsaber glanced against his wrist. The burn was nothing compared to his annoyance at himself.

"Round three, it is," Yoda called from the sidelines. "Approach from opposite corners, you should."

Qui-Gon wiped his forehead with his sleeve. When he had agreed to take part in a training exercise with the advanced Temple students, he hadn't expected to work so hard.

He could hear the murmur from the student onlookers as Bruck Chun bowed and retreated to his corner. Bruck was doing better than anyone had expected. He had made it through all six rounds with different opponents. This would be his final match.

Qui-Gon remembered Bruck from his last visit to the Temple. The white-haired boy had fought Obi-Wan in a tough, long match. The two boys were fierce rivals. They had fought out of fury at each other and a desire to win Qui-Gon's approval. Qui-Gon had been impressed with Obi-Wan's skills, but not with his anger. Watching Obi-Wan fight, Qui-Gon had been determined not to take the promising boy as his Padawan.

Why hadn't he listened to his instincts?

Qui-Gon wrenched his attention to the present moment. He must concentrate. Bruck's fighting skills had improved tremendously. The duel should have been easy for Qui-Gon, but he found his distraction harder to fight. Bruck had surprised Qui-Gon more than once. The boy fought doggedly, never tiring, and was quick to take advantage of Qui-Gon's lapses in concentration.

Bruck circled him, his lightsaber held in a defensive attitude. The training sabers were set on low power. A blow would cause a sting, not an injury. Blocks littered the floor to make the ground uneven. The lights were kept at half-power to add to the difficulty. A blow to the neck would declare the winner.

Qui-Gon watched, waiting for Bruck to make his next move. Bruck began to fade to the left. Qui-Gon noted how his hands tightened on his lightsaber. Impatience had always been Bruck's weakness, just as it was Obi-Wan's. . . .

Was his former Padawan's impatience getting him in trouble back on the treacherous world of Melida/Daan?

Too late, Qui-Gon saw the flash of the lightsaber. Bruck had utilized a simple trick, a trick that never should have fooled him. He had reversed direction. The blow came down as Bruck leaped into the air, twisting to come at Qui-Gon's opposite side. The blow missed Qui-Gon's neck by a hair. Qui-Gon ducked, and took the blow hard on his shoulder. As he staggered, he heard the onlookers gasp.

He'd had enough of this. He was tired of his own inattention. It was time to end it.

Qui-Gon allowed his body to ease into his misstep, fooling Bruck. The boy came at him too eagerly, his balance off. Qui-Gon whirled

and attacked. Bruck stumbled backward, surprised. He flailed at Qui-Gon with his lightsaber.
Another mistake. Qui-Gon's next blow had all
his weight behind it. Bruck nearly dropped his
lightsaber.

Qui-Gon pushed his advantage. He attacked,
his lightsaber now just a blur in the dusky light.
Slashing, parrying, whirling to come at Bruck
from yet another angle, then another, Qui-Gon
forced the boy back into a corner. Now the mur-
murs he heard from the onlookers were of ap-
preciation for the skill of a Jedi Master. Qui-Gon
tuned them out. The battle was not over until
the final defeat.

Bruck tried a last assault, but the boy was
tired. It was not hard for Qui-Gon to knock
Bruck's weapon from his hand and lightly touch
the end of his own lightsaber to the boy's neck.

"End point, it is," Yoda announced.

The two exchanged the ritual bows and the
customary eye contact. At the end of every
match, each Jedi showed respect to the other
and gratitude for his lesson, win or lose. Qui-
Gon had fought many times in this way.
Sometimes, Jedi students could not control
their frustration or anger during the ritual bow.

But in Bruck's steady gaze Qui-Gon saw only
respect. That was an improvement.

But he saw other things. Curiosity. Desire.

Bruck was going to be thirteen in a few days. He had not yet been chosen as a Padawan. Time was running out. He was most likely wondering if Qui-Gon would choose him.

Everyone was wondering, Qui-Gon knew. Teachers, students, even the Council. Why had he returned to the Temple? Had he come to choose another apprentice?

Qui-Gon turned away from the speculation in Bruck's eyes. He would never choose a Padawan again.

He returned his lightsaber to his belt. Bruck replaced his in the rack where the senior students left their weapons after training. Qui-Gon quickly walked through the dressing and washing rooms and activated the door to the Room of a Thousand Fountains.

He felt the coolness of the air with relief. Here in the enormous greenhouse it was always refreshing. The sound of rushing water and the many shades of green soothed a restless spirit. He could hear the trickle of the small fountains nestled in the ferns, as well as the gentle thunder of the larger waterfalls down the paths. Qui-Gon had always found the garden peaceful. He hoped that now it would calm his raging heart.

Privacy was greatly respected at the Temple.

Qui-Gon had not been confronted with questions since he'd arrived. Yet he knew that curiosity bubbled beneath the calm surface of the Temple just as the hidden fountains flowed in the gardens. Students and teachers alike wanted to know the answer to one question: What had gone wrong between him and his Padawan, Obi-Wan Kenobi?

Even if someone asked him the question, would he be able to answer it? Qui-Gon sighed. The situation whirled with cloudy motivations and uncertain paths. Had he misjudged his Padawan? Had he been too firm with Obi-Wan? Not firm enough?

Qui-Gon didn't have an answer. All he knew was that Obi-Wan had made an astonishing and bewildering choice. He had thrown away his Jedi training like it was a worn-out tunic.

"Troubled you are, if the garden you seek," Yoda said from behind him.

Qui-Gon turned. "Not troubled. Just overheated from the battle."

Yoda gave a slight nod. He did not fully respond if he felt a Jedi had dodged an issue. Qui-Gon knew that well.

"Avoiding me, you have been," Yoda remarked. He settled himself on a stone bench placed near a fountain that ran over smooth white pebbles. The sound of the water was nearly music.

"I've been watching over Tahl," Qui-Gon answered.

Tahl was the Jedi Knight who Qui-Gon and Obi-Wan had rescued from Melida/Daan. She had been blinded in an attack and then held as a prisoner of war.

Again, Yoda only nodded slightly. "Better healers we have at the Temple than you," he said. "And in need of constant care, Tahl is not. Welcomes it not, I think."

Qui-Gon could not suppress a half smile. It was true. Tahl was already impatient with the constant attention. She didn't like to be fussed over.

"Time it is for you to speak your heart," Yoda said softly. "Past time, it is."

With a heavy sigh, Qui-Gon sat on the bench next to Yoda. He did not want to unburden his heart. Yet Yoda had a right to know the facts.

"He stayed," Qui-Gon said simply. "He told me he had found something on Melida/Daan that was more important than his Jedi training. On the morning we were leaving, the Elders attacked the Young. They had starfighters and weapons. The Young were disorganized. They needed help."

"And yet stay you did not."

"My orders were to return to the Temple with Tahl."

Yoda leaned slightly backward in surprise. "Orders, they were? Counsel, it was. And always willing to ignore my counsel you are, if suits you it does."

Qui-Gon gave a start. Obi-Wan had flung almost the same words at him back on Melida/Daan.

"Are you saying I should have stayed?" Qui-Gon asked irritably. "What if Tahl had died?"

Yoda sighed. "A hard choice it was, Qui-Gon. Yet willing are you to blame your Padawan. Place the choice before him you did: forsake Jedi training, or children die, friends are betrayed. Thought you understood a boy's heart, I did."

Qui-Gon stared stonily ahead. He had not expected this rebuke from Yoda.

"Impulsive you were yourself as a student," Yoda continued. "Led by the heart, many times you were. And wrong, many times you were as well. This I remember."

"I never would have left the Jedi," Qui-Gon said angrily.

"True that is," Yoda said, nodding in agreement. "Commitment you had. Absolute it was. Does this mean that to question, others must not? Like you always, they must be?"

Qui-Gon shifted on the bench. These conversations with Yoda could be painful. The Jedi Master had a way of poking the deepest wound.

"So I should let him make his foolish decision," Qui-Gon said with a shrug. "Let him fight a war he can't win. Let him stand and watch the massacre that will result. He'll be lucky if he escapes with his life."

"Ah, see I do." Yoda's yellow eyes gleamed. "Unbiased by your feeling, your prediction is?"

Qui-Gon nodded shortly. "I see disaster there. The Young cannot win."

"Interesting," Yoda murmured. "For win they did, Qui-Gon."

Qui-Gon turned to him, startled.

"Word we have received," Yoda said calmly. "Won the war, the Young have. Forming a government, they are. Understand now do you, Obi-Wan's decision? Fighting for a lost cause, he was not. A planet ruler, he has become."

Hiding his surprise, Qui-Gon turned away. "Then he is more foolish than I thought," he coolly replied.

CHAPTER 3

Obi-Wan sat between Nield and Cerasi at a huge round conference table. The Young had taken over the bombed-out Melida/Daan Unified Congress Building. It had stood intact for only three years, during a period where the Melida and Daan had tried to rule together before war had broken out again.

The Young had taken it over as a symbolic gesture of unity. There were certainly more welcoming places they could have chosen. They had tried to clear most of the rubble, but they were forced to leave the heavier fallen beams and columns. The windows had been blown out, and more than half the roof was gone.

Obi-Wan was damp and cold and uncomfortable, but he was thrilled to be here, forming a new government. The days were long and difficult, but he never felt tired. There was so much to think about and so much to do.

The Young had won the war. But the hard part was just beginning. Before, they had all been in agreement. They had simply wanted peace. But now the Young waged a war of words among themselves. There were too many decisions to make and too many opinions.

The city of Zehava was a ruin. Many people did not have heat, and food was scarce. Hospitals needed supplies. Fuel for floaters and transports was low. But the worst problem was the amount of arms still carried by the citizens, most of them former soldiers. Tensions ran high, and any small conflict could escalate into a serious battle.

The Young were in the majority on Melida/Daan, especially since the decimated Middle Generation had thrown their support to them during the war. It had been easy to reach an agreement to elect Nield as temporary governor. In addition, an advisory council of ten members had been set up. Obi-Wan was on it, along with Mawat and other Young leaders. Cerasi headed the council. As governor, Nield was required to follow any motion that was voted by a majority. He cast one vote as well.

Nield and the council had gone to work immediately, forming squads to address the separate problems that Zehava faced. Obi-Wan was head of the Security Squad. It was the most dangerous duty, involving a house-to-house weapons sweep of the entire city. Until further notice, only members of the Security Squad were allowed to carry weapons. All others were directed to turn their weapons in to a warehouse until the tensions eased. Obi-Wan had not been surprised when many people did not want to cooperate. Even some of the Young were reluctant to hand over their weapons. They had all lived with conflict for too long.

The policy had been discussed at the first general meeting. There had been shouting and furious arguments.

Cerasi had faced them all down. She had stood in the middle of the ruined building and seemed to meet every eye in the packed house. "Peace isn't just a concept to me," she had said. "It is life and breath. I will never pick up a weapon again. I have seen what they can do. If a weapon of destruction is in my hands, sooner or later that weapon will be used. I will not contribute to one more death on Melida/Daan!"

After a silence, the Young had burst into cheers. Cerasi had flushed with happiness and pride as boys and girls streamed up to the council table and handed over their weapons. It had been a proud moment.

"First order of business," Cerasi now said crisply, breaking into Obi-Wan's thoughts.

"Let's get progress reports from the squad heads. Nield, would you begin?"

Nield stood. He was head of the New History Squad, which was in charge of demolishing the symbols of hatred and division in Zehava — war monuments, military statues, and the great Halls of Evidence, which housed holograms of warriors telling tales of hatred and bloodshed.

"As you all know," Nield began in a ringing voice, "the building of a new society can only take place if the old rivalries are stamped out. How can the fragile peace hold if both Melida and Daan still have places to go to fuel their hatred? I say that the destruction of the Halls of Evidence should be our first priority!"

Many onlookers cheered. But Taun, the head of the Utilities Squad, in charge of bringing back power and heat to the many ruined buildings, raised his hand.

"The people are cold and hungry," he said. "Isn't helping them more important?"

"It's when they're cold and hungry that they blame the other side," Nield answered. "That's when the lines at the Halls of Evidence grow long. People would rather warm themselves with hatred than blankets."

"What about the med centers?" Dor, a quiet boy, spoke up. "The sick can't line up at the Halls. They need medicine."

"And the orphans?" someone else called. "The care centers can't handle the overflow."

"I would say that rebuilding housing is our first priority," Nena, the head of the Housing Squad, spoke up. "There are so many who were displaced by the war."

Nield suddenly brought his hand down on the table with a sharp *crack.* The buzz of conversation stopped.

"All of these problems come from the endless wars!" he cried. "And the endless wars spring from the endless hate! We *must* destroy the Halls first. It will give the people hope. Hope that we can bury the past as easily as we bury the symbols of our division!"

A hush fell on the room. Everyone stared at Nield. His words rang true.

"I know destroying the resting places of our ancestors is asking people to sacrifice their memories," Nield continued. "That is why I've chosen the resting place of my ancestors as the first Hall to be demolished. I want to remember my parents as *people.* Not warriors! I want to remember them with *love.* Not hate! Come with me now," he urged, leaning over the table, his voice carrying to every corner of the room. "Let me show you what a great mark of unity this will be. Are you with me?"

"We're with you!" the Young shouted.

Nield sprang up and strode down the center aisle. "Then come on!"

Boys and girls jumped up and ran behind him, cheering. Grinning, Obi-Wan and Cerasi followed.

"Nield will always be able to bring us together," Cerasi exclaimed, her face glowing.

The crowd followed Nield to the Daan sector, where a huge Hall of Evidence was located on a large, glittering blue lake. The low black structure hovered on repulsorlifts, covering almost the entire surface of the lake.

Already, workers from Nield's squad were carrying out the stone markers on small speeders. They dumped them in a growing pile.

Mawat waved Nield over as soon as the crowd arrived. "Hey, I made sure they saved these intact," he told Nield in a low voice. "I didn't know if you wanted to keep them."

Obi-Wan looked over at the stone markers. He saw the name MICAE chiseled on one, with the warrior's birth and death dates. Next to it was a marker for Leidra. They were Nield's parents.

Nield looked down at the markers. "I'm glad you saved them," he murmured to Mawat.

Obi-Wan exchanged a surprised glance with Cerasi. Would Nield reconsider his position now that he was face-to-face with the last evidence of his parents?

Nield caressed the golden globe that activated the projection. His father appeared in hologram form, brandishing a blaster and wearing armor.

"I am Micae, son of Terandi of Garth, from the North Country," the hologram began.

Nield turned and activated the hologram of his mother, Leidra. A tall woman with Nield's dark eyes appeared. "I am Leidra, wife of Micae, daughter of Pei of Quadri," she began.

The two voices combined, each drowning out the other. Obi-Wan could pick out isolated words and phrases about battles fought and won, ancestors dead, villages destroyed.

Nield picked up a beamdrill. Now the crowd had gathered around him. A solemn look was on his face as he turned to the marker for his father.

"I was but a boy when the evil Melida invaded Garth and herded my people into camps," Micae was saying. "There —"

Nield attacked the marker with the beamdrill, shattering it into pieces. The hologram dissolved into glittering fragments, then disappeared.

Only the voice of Nield's mother remained.

"And to my son, Nield, my treasure, my hope, I leave my love and my undying hatred for the filthy Melida —"

Leidra's voice was cut off as Nield set to work on her marker. The hologram wavered, then dissolved. The harsh sound of the beamdrill filled the air. Stone splintered and chips flew, cutting Nield on his arms. He didn't seem to feel it. He operated the drill until his parents' markers were ground to small chunks of stone.

"Now they are gone forever," Cerasi whispered. Obi-Wan saw a small tear trickle down from the corner of her eye.

Nield turned. He wiped the sweat from his brow with a forearm. Blood from his cuts mingled with the dust covering his face. He leaned down to pick up one of the chunks of stone. He held it aloft.

"The remnants of these stones will be used to build new housing for Melida and Daan to live together in peace," he shouted. "Today, a new history is born!"

A great roar rose from the crowd. Many rushed into the Hall to help dismantle it. Others hoisted pieces of stone and cheered.

Obi-Wan stood next to Nield and Cerasi. It was a historic moment. He had helped to shape it.

He had no regrets about leaving the Jedi. He was home.

CHAPTER 4

Qui-Gon was in his quarters when he got the message that he was to report to the Jedi Council immediately. He was most likely being called to report on what had happened with Obi-Wan.

He rose with a sigh. He had returned to the Temple for peace. Instead, he was forced to re-live the situation over and over.

Still, a request from the Council could not be ignored. Part of being a Jedi was recognizing that one's own wisdom had limits. The Council was made up of the wisest and best of the Jedi Masters. If they wanted to hear from Qui-Gon directly, he would tell them.

Qui-Gon entered the Council room. It was the highest room in one of the Temple towers, tak-ing up the entire top story. Outside the windows that ran from floor to ceiling, the spires and towers of Coruscant hovered below. The sun was just rising, brushing the clouds with orange fire.

Qui-Gon stood in the center of the room, bowed respectfully, and waited. How would they begin? Would Mace Windu, whose dark eyes could burn through you like hot coals, demand his reason for leaving a thirteen-year-old boy in the middle of a war? Would Saesee Tiin murmur that Qui-Gon's actions had always come from an impulsive but giving heart? He had been called before the Council more than most Knights. He could guess at what each would say.

Yoda began the meeting. "Call you here on a matter of grave importance we have. Secret it is. A series of thefts we have discovered."

Qui-Gon was startled. He had not been prepared for this. "Here at the Temple?"

Yoda nodded. "Sorry I am to report such a thing. Taken are things that do not have monetary value. Yet serious the thefts are. Against the Jedi Code, they are."

"Does the Council believe that a student is responsible?" Qui-Gon asked, frowning. Such a thing was unheard of at the Temple.

"This we do not know," Yoda replied.

"If it is not, then some outside force has invaded the Temple. Either possibility is intolerable," Mace Windu put in. "And both must be investigated." He knit his long, elegant fingers together. "That is why we've called you here, Qui-Gon. We need to investigate discreetly. We don't want to alarm the youngest students, or tip off the thief. We'd like you to take charge of the investigation."

"Work with Tahl, you will," Yoda added. "True it is that she cannot see. But remarkable are her powers."

Qui-Gon nodded. He agreed with Yoda. Tahl's intuition and intelligence were renowned.

"The thefts may seem small for now," Mace Windu warned. "But a small threat can be a hint of a greater threat to come. Either from within or without, this threat is real. Take care, Qui-Gon."

"Yes, I heard," Tahl told Qui-Gon when he came to see her in her quarters. "Yoda came to see me this morning. Woke me up with bad news. Not my favorite way to start the day."

Tahl gave an ironic half smile, one that Qui-Gon knew well. They had gone through Temple training together. Tahl had always attracted notice. Strong and beautiful, with skin the color of dark honey and striped green and gold eyes, Tahl and her sharp tongue had deflated pride and exposed bullies, even as a six-year-old.

Now when he saw her sightless eyes and the

white scar that ran from her left eyebrow to her chin, Qui-Gon's heart contracted in pain. Tahl was still gloriously beautiful, but it hurt to see the visible signs of how she had suffered.

"I heard the healers were with you yesterday," Qui-Gon remarked.

"Yes, that was another reason that Yoda came to me. He wanted to make sure I was all right," Tahl said. The half smile quirked a corner of her mouth. "Yesterday I was told that I would never have sight again."

The bad news made Qui-Gon slowly sink down into a chair next to her. He was glad she could not see the pain on his face. "I'm sorry." He had been hoping, along with Tahl, that the healers on Coruscant would be able to restore her sight.

She shrugged. "Yoda came to tell me I was needed on this investigation. I think that our friend gave me this assignment so that I can turn my mind to other things."

"If you would rather not, I can find another partner," Qui-Gon said. "The Council will understand."

She gave his hand a pat and reached for the teapot. "No, Qui-Gon. Yoda is right, as he always is. And if there is a threat to the Temple, I want to help. Now have some tea." She felt the pot. "It's still warm."

"Let me," Qui-Gon said quickly.

"No," Tahl said sharply. "I must do things for myself. If we're going to work together, you have to understand that."

Qui-Gon nodded, then realized she couldn't see him. He would have to get used to this new Tahl. She might have lost her sight, but her perception was stronger than ever.

"All right," he said mildly. "I'd like some tea."

Tahl reached out for a cup. "Don't you know what I've been up to these past weeks? Training exercises. I'm working with the Masters to develop my hearing, sense of smell, and touch. I've already made some remarkable progress. I had no idea how sharp my hearing could be."

"And here I thought it was your tongue that was sharp," Qui-Gon said.

She laughed as she steadied the cup with one hand and began to pour. "And Yoda arranged a surprise for me. An unwelcome surprise, I must say, but don't ever tell him. He —"

"One centimeter to the left!" A musical voice rang out from behind them suddenly. Startled, Tahl spilled the tea on her wrist.

"Stars and galaxies!" she cried.

Qui-Gon handed her a napkin. He turned to see a droid roll into the room. It had the silver body shell of a protocol droid, but Qui-Gon could see that other features had been included. Extra sensors were built into the head, and the arms were longer. Now they shot out and took the cup from Tahl.

"You see, Master Tahl, you spilled the tea," the droid said.

"I spilled it because you startled me, you hunk of recycled tin," Tahl sputtered. "And don't call me Master Tahl."

"Yes, certainly, sir," the droid replied.

"I'm not a sir. I'm a female. Who's the blind one here?"

Qui-Gon tried to hide his grin. "What's this?" he asked, indicating the droid.

"Meet Yoda's surprise," Tahl said with a grimace. "2JTJ, but call it TooJay. It's a personal navigation droid. It's supposed to help me with domestic matters until I can navigate alone. It scans for obstructions and I can program it to lead me to any destination."

"Seems like a good idea," Qui-Gon remarked as TooJay efficiently cleaned up the spill and poured more tea.

"I'd rather walk into walls," Tahl grumbled. "It's thoughtful of Yoda, but I'm not used to having a constant companion. I never did take a Padawan."

Qui-Gon sipped his tea. Once he had felt as Tahl did. He hadn't wanted a Padawan after his first, Xanatos, had destroyed every bond of honor and loyalty between them. He enjoyed being alone. He liked being responsible for only himself. Then Obi-Wan had come into his life. He had grown used to having him there.

"I'm sorry, Qui-Gon," Tahl said gently. "That was a careless remark. I know you miss Obi-Wan."

Carefully, Qui-Gon set down his cup. "If I am not to help you pour the tea, then can I request that you not tell me how I am feeling?"

"Well, perhaps you don't know that you miss him," Tahl said. "But you do."

Annoyed, Qui-Gon stood. "Do you forget what he did? He stole the starfighter to destroy those deflection towers. If he had been shot down, you would have died on Melida/Daan!"

"Ah, so you have a new talent. You can see things that might have been. Must come in handy."

Qui-Gon paced in front of her. "He would have stolen it again, if I hadn't stopped him. He would have left us on that planet with no way to get off."

Tahl pushed Qui-Gon's chair out with her foot. "Sit down, Qui-Gon. I can't see you, but you're making me nervous. If I don't blame Obi-Wan, why should you? It's my life you're talking about."

Qui-Gon didn't sit, but he did stop pacing. Tahl cocked her head, trying to gauge his mood.

"It was a tough call," she said in a gentler tone. "You went one way, Obi-Wan another. It seems to me that you're the only one who continues to blame the boy. And he is a boy, Qui-Gon. Remember that."

Qui-Gon was silent. Once again, he found himself discussing Obi-Wan. And he didn't want to discuss his Padawan with Tahl, or even Yoda. No one knew how much of himself he had invested in the boy in such a short time. No one knew how Obi-Wan's decision had grieved him.

"Maybe we should talk about the investigation," he said finally. "It's a high priority. We're wasting time."

"True," Tahl said, nodding. "I think the Council is right. We can't treat this lightly. There is danger here."

"Where should we start?" Qui-Gon asked, sitting down. "Do you have any ideas?"

"One of the thefts was in a semi-restricted area," Tahl pointed out. "Some student records are missing. Let's see who has access to the Temple registry. When you don't know where to begin, the obvious is a good place to start."

CHAPTER 5

Obi-Wan strapped a blaster to his hip and made sure his vibroblade was in its holster. He had received a report of holdouts in the Melida sector who had refused to turn over their weapons.

He, Cerasi, and Nield were still living in the Young's underground vault until accommodations could be found. It wouldn't be right to take housing when so many were without. He walked out into the main vault where his Security Squad waited. He nodded at Deila, his second in command. They were ready.

They climbed up a ladder to a grate and hoisted themselves onto the street. They had gone only a few steps when Obi-Wan heard the sound of running footsteps behind him. He turned and saw Cerasi.

"I heard about the holdouts," she said as she

ran up, fastening her warm hooded tunic. "I'm coming with you."

Obi-Wan shook his head. "Cerasi, this could be dangerous."

Her green eyes glinted. "Oh, and the war we fought together wasn't?"

"You don't carry a weapon," Obi-Wan said, exasperated. "There could be shooting."

"Relax, Obi-Wan," Cerasi said, buckling a thick belt around her waist. "I have my own bag of tricks."

Despite his worry, Obi-Wan couldn't help smiling. Cerasi had devised a number of trick "weapons." They were slingshots that gave off the sound of blaster fire.

"All right," he agreed. "But for once, follow my orders, will you?"

"Yes, Captain," Cerasi teased.

It was a cold day, and their breath mingled as it clouded the air. They passed a square where some members of the New History Squad were busy dismantling a war monument. A group of Melida Elders watched, their faces stony.

"They expect us to put up monuments to ourselves, I hear," Cerasi said. "I can't wait to surprise them. No more war memorials on Melida/Daan."

"Are you sure?" Obi-Wan asked with a

straight face. "I can see you up on a pedestal holding up your slingshot —"

Cerasi nudged him with her shoulder. "Watch it, friend." She grinned at him. "I didn't know Jedi were allowed to joke."

"Of course we are." Obi-Wan's face flushed. "I mean, they are." He spoke lightly, but a shadow must have crossed his face because the smile left Cerasi's lips.

"You gave up so much for us," she said sadly.

"And look what I received," Obi-Wan replied, swinging his arm to encompass Zehava.

Laughter bubbled out from Cerasi. "Sure. A destroyed city, bad food, no heat, a home in a tunnel, a job disarming fanatics, and —"

"Friends," Obi-Wan finished.

Cerasi smiled. "Friends."

The large, two-story building where some of the Melida holdouts were living seemed peaceful under the sharp blue sky. It looked perfectly intact from the front, but as they carefully circled it, keeping out of sight, they saw that the back had been completely demolished. A repair job had been attempted with a combination of boards and tough plastoid sheets.

There was one thing odd about the house, Obi-Wan noted. There was no back door. He pointed it out to Cerasi.

"Only one entrance to defend," she said,

squinting up at the roof. "That way we can't surprise them."

"I don't want to surprise them," Obi-Wan said. "I have to give them the chance to surrender their arms. I can't go in shooting." He looked at the house, his hand drifting toward his belt. It was still a surprise to feel a vibroblade there instead of a lightsaber.

"We need a lookout on the street," Obi-Wan continued. "That's you."

For a moment, Cerasi seemed about to protest. Then she nodded. She held out her hand, palm out. Obi-Wan put his up against hers, as close as he could without touching.

"Good luck."

"We don't need luck."

"Everybody needs luck."

"Not us."

Obi-Wan ducked around the corner, followed by his squad of six boys and girls, the best fighters the Young had.

He knocked on the door. He heard movement behind it, but nothing happened. He leaned closer to the door and shouted, "We are the Young Security Squad. You are ordered by the acting governor of Melida/Daan to open the door."

"Come back when your voice changes," someone shouted from inside.

Obi-Wan sighed. He had been hoping for co-operation. He nodded at Deila, their explosives expert. She quickly set explosive charges near the lock of the heavy door.

"Stand back from the door," she shouted to those inside.

The Security Squad had done this before. Many Melida and Daan Elders would not open their doors to them or recognize their authority. This was a quick way to show them who was in charge. No lives were lost — just doors.

Deila motioned to all of them to step back, then set the charge and jumped back with them. A muffled *boom* split the silence. The door shook. Deila stepped forward and nudged it with a toe. It fell with a loud *thud,* and the Security Squad rushed in, with Obi-Wan leading the charge.

At first, he couldn't see anything. But he hadn't forgotten his Jedi training. He let go of the urgent need to see and accepted the darkness. In only seconds, he could make out shapes.

Shapes with weapons . . .

The Melida Elders stood at the end of the long hallway. Their backs were to a stairway leading upward. They all wore battered plastoid armor and held their weapons pointed at the squad.

Obi-Wan saw his problem at once. He would

have to end the conflict here. The group had access to the stairway. More lives could be lost if his squad was forced to follow them upstairs. There could be booby traps. At the very least, it would be a dangerous exercise to try to locate all six Elders upstairs.

One of them spoke. "We do not recognize your authority."

Obi-Wan knew the voice. It belonged to Wehutti, Cerasi's father. Cerasi had not seen him in years. Obi-Wan was glad that she was outside.

"It doesn't matter if you don't recognize it," Obi-Wan answered in a steady tone. "We have it. You lost the war. We've formed a new government."

"I do not recognize your government!" Wehutti cried sharply. His powerful hand gripped a blaster. He had lost his other arm in an earlier war, but Obi-Wan had seen firsthand that Wehutti could inflict more damage with one arm than most warriors could with two.

"Young fools!" Wehutti continued harshly. "You talk of peace with weapons in your hands! You are no different from us. You wage war to get what you want. You oppress the people to keep what you have. You are hypocrites and fools. Why should we bend to your authority?"

Obi-Wan began to walk forward. His squad

followed him. "Drop your weapons or we'll arrest you. We've called for reinforcements."

At least he hoped so. The standard operating procedure was for the last one in to signal the lookout to call if it looked as if there would be resistance. Cerasi should have contacted Mawat on her comlink by now.

"If you take another step, Jedi, I'll fire," Wehutti said, leveling his blaster.

Before Obi-Wan could take his next step, blaster fire erupted from upstairs. Obi-Wan sprang backward to avoid it, but he couldn't see where it was coming from.

Wehutti sprang backward as well. That meant that he didn't know where it was coming from, either.

Cerasi! Somehow she had climbed into the upper story. Cerasi was an agile, fearless gymnast. She had pulled what she called a "rooftop special," jumping from an adjoining roof onto another and then swinging down to a window.

Obi-Wan took advantage of Wehutti's surprise and launched himself at the group, his squad on his heels. He leaped into the air, twisting his body in order to bring the hilt of his vibroblade down on Wehutti's wrist. Even a powerful man like Wehutti couldn't withstand the shock of such a blow. He howled and dropped his blaster.

Obi-Wan scooped it up as he whirled to disarm the next Elder. He saw a flash of movement behind him. It was Cerasi, leaping over the stairway rail into the fray. She dove feetfirst into a Melida Elder. The Elder's vibro-ax clattered to the floor, and Deila picked it up.

Within thirty seconds, the entire group was disarmed.

"Thank you for your cooperation," Obi-Wan said. It had been decided that if resisters were disarmed without any loss of life, no one would be arrested. If they had to arrest every resister, Nield pointed out, they would have no place to put them.

"A curse on the foul Youth who destroy our civilization!" Wehutti spat out. His green eyes were similar in color to Cerasi's, but they blazed with hate.

Cerasi stood rooted to the spot, transfixed by her father's hatred. He had not recognized the slight figure in the brown cloak and hood.

Obi-Wan tugged on her arm, and she followed him outside. The cold air cooled their flushed cheeks.

"Deila, take the weapons back to the warehouse," Obi-Wan said wearily. "We'll take a break for now."

Deila waved. "Good work, chief."

The rest of the squad headed off. Cerasi

walked in silence next to Obi-Wan for a few minutes. It was cold, and they tucked their hands inside their cloaks for warmth.

"I'm sorry I didn't call for reinforcements," Cerasi said. "I figured we could handle it."

"Did you know Wehutti was there?" Obi-Wan asked.

"Not for sure. But when I hear about a bunch of stubborn angry Melida holdouts, naturally my dear dad springs to mind."

Cerasi tilted her face back to catch the warming rays of the sun. She looked serene, but Obi-Wan had picked up the sad bitterness in her voice.

"He is wrong," Obi-Wan admitted quietly. "But he knows no other way."

"I was stupid enough to think this war would change him." Cerasi stooped down to pick up a piece of rubble in her path. She threw it into a pile at the side of the road and tucked her hand inside again. "I thought if we survived the last war we'd ever fight on Melida/Daan, we'd find each other again. Stupid."

"Not stupid," Obi-Wan said carefully. "Maybe it just hasn't happened yet."

"It's funny, Obi-Wan," Cerasi said thoughtfully. "I had no empty places inside me during the war. I was filled up with my desire for peace, my friendships with the Young. Now we have victory, and my heart feels empty. I didn't think I would miss my family ever again. But now I want something to connect to that goes as deep as blood."

Obi-Wan swallowed. Cerasi continually surprised him. Every time he thought he knew her, another layer would peel back, and he would see a different person. He had met a tough, angry girl who could shoot and fight almost as skillfully as a Jedi. After the war, he had seen an idealist emerge with the power to move hearts and minds. Now he saw a young girl who just wanted a home.

"You connect to me, Cerasi," he said. "You've changed me. We support each other and protect each other. That's family, right?"

"I guess."

He stopped and turned to face her. "We'll be each other's family." He held up his hand. This time, she pressed her palm against it.

The wind picked up, cutting through their cloaks and making them shiver. Still, they kept their palms together. Obi-Wan felt the warmth of Cerasi's skin. He could almost feel the beating of her blood against his.

"You see," he said, "I have lost everything, too."

CHAPTER 6

A tool box from the servo-utility unit
Holographic files and computer records for students with names A through H
A teacher's meditation robe
A fourth-year student's sports activity kit

Qui-Gon stared at the list. It was such an odd assortment of items. He could see no pattern there. He and Tahl were working on the assumption that these were petty thefts. That would be the easy answer. Somewhere there could be a student who seemed to be adjusting but who was hiding resentment or anger. He or she had lashed out.

But Qui-Gon had learned through long experience that the easy answer usually just led to a harder question.

The holographic files on the students were

kept by Jedi Master T'un. T'un had a record of long years of service. He was several hundred years old, a wizened being of great learning. He had kept the records of the Temple for the past fifty years. Each year he was aided by two student helpers who volunteered for service. Tahl and Qui-Gon had interviewed both of them. They had answered steadily and clearly. Only T'un and other members of the Council had access to the private files. The students were never alone in the filing office without T'un.

It was typical of their investigation. Every lead had turned into a dead end.

An urgent knock came on his door. "Qui-Gon," Tahl called softly. "I need you."

He opened the door. "More bad news," she said with an anxious frown. "The senior training rooms have been vandalized. All of the lightsabers have been stolen."

Dismay made him slow to respond. Obi-Wan's lightsaber had been in the senior training room. Qui-Gon had left it there. Part of him had hoped that someday Obi-Wan would reclaim it.

"This is no longer petty theft," he said.

"Yoda has cordoned off the room until we see it," Tahl explained. "Hurry, before TooJay catches up with me."

They walked quickly to the lift tube and took it

to the training floor. Qui-Gon strode into the changing rooms. He stopped short, and Tahl bumped into him from behind.

"What is it?" she asked. "What do you see?"

Qui-Gon couldn't answer for a moment. Sick at heart, he surveyed the room. Training tunics had been ripped to shreds, the pieces flung around the room. Lockers were flung open, their contents spilled onto the floor.

"I can feel it," Tahl said. "Anger. Destruction." She picked her way through the debris, reaching down to pick up a scrap of fabric. "What else?"

"A message," Qui-Gon said. "Scrawled on the wall in red." He read it to her.

> COME, YOUR TIME WILL
> BEWARE YOU MUST, TROUBLE I AM

"It's mocking Yoda," she said. "I know the students imitate him sometimes. Even I do. But we do it with great affection. Qui-Gon, there is hate here."

"Yes."

"We have to get to the bottom of this. And the students must know. We must go on alert."

"Yes," he agreed. "This cannot be secret any longer."

*   *   *

The Temple went on high-security alert. It was a decision the Council was reluctant to make. It made prisoners out of the students. They needed passes to leave the Temple, passes to use the gardens and to swim in the lake. They needed to account for their time at every minute of the day. It was for everyone's protection, but it violated the spirit of the Temple. The Temple's philosophy was that discipline needed to come from within. Security checks contradicted that concept.

But Qui-Gon and Tahl had insisted on the measure, and Yoda had agreed. The safety of the students was their primary concern.

An atmosphere of mistrust grew at the Temple. Students eyed each other with suspicion. As they were called into interviews with Qui-Gon and Tahl, they watched each other for guilty signs. Yet no one could believe that a student could be capable of such vandalism.

Bruck was one such student. "I know it can't be any of the senior students," he told Tahl and Qui-Gon quietly when they called on him. "We have been through training together. I can't imagine any one of us wanting to damage the Temple."

"It's hard to see into another person's heart," Qui-Gon remarked.

"I was the last person to leave the training rooms last night," Bruck said. "And of course you know that months ago I was disciplined for my anger. I've worked with Yoda, and I've made progress. But I guess I'm still a suspect." Bruck met Qui-Gon's gaze steadily.

"We suspect no one as yet," Tahl assured him. "Did you see anything odd last night? Think carefully."

Bruck closed his eyes for a long moment. "Nothing," he said finally. "I powered down the lights, and I left. We never lock the training rooms. I took the turbolift to the dining hall. I was with my friends all evening until bed."

Qui-Gon nodded. He had already confirmed Bruck's story.

He and Tahl weren't even certain what they were looking for. They were merely gathering information, trying to see if the students had seen anything out of the ordinary, even if it didn't seem to be important at the time.

They dismissed Bruck, and Tahl turned to Qui-Gon with a sigh. "I think he's right. I can't imagine any of the senior students doing this. They are Jedi."

Qui-Gon passed a weary hand over his forehead. "And no one has heard of a student who has recently been angry or upset. Just the usual things — a bad performance on an exercise, or a petty disagreement . . ." He drummed on the table, thinking. "Yet Bruck was angry once."

"Yoda says he's made great improvements," Tahl said. "And Bruck acknowledged his problem used to be anger. He admitted it must look bad for him that he was the last one to use the room. I got no sense of darkness from him. A boy so honest couldn't have done this."

"Unless he was very, very clever," Qui-Gon remarked.

"Do you suspect him?"

"No," Qui-Gon said. "I suspect no one and everyone . . ."

"Master Tahl!" TooJay suddenly appeared in the doorway of the interview room. "I am here to lead you to the dining hall."

Tahl gritted her teeth. "I'm busy."

"It is dinnertime," TooJay said in a musical tone.

"I can find it," Tahl snapped.

"It is five levels down —"

"I know where it is!"

"There is a datapad three centimeters to your left —"

"I know! And in another second, it will be flying at your head!"

"I see you are busy. I will return." TooJay beeped at them in a friendly way, and scooted off.

Tahl dropped her head in her hands. "Remind me to get a pair of vibro-cutters, will you, Qui-Gon? I really need to dismantle that droid." With a heavy sigh, she raised her head. "This investigation will try the nerves of everyone at the Temple. I feel a serious disturbance in the Force."

"I do as well."

"I fear it is not a student who is doing this. I think it's an invader. Someone who hates us. Someone who wants to see us fractured and distracted . . ."

"Someone who could have a larger plan in mind, you mean? Is that what you're afraid of?"

Tahl turned her worried emerald and gold eyes to him. "It is what I fear the most," she said.

"As do I," Qui-Gon softly replied.

CHAPTER 7

Obi-Wan walked through the city streets, exhausted. He had just finished three solid days of Security Squad duty. It had been hard, but they had managed to disarm whole quadrants of the city. There were only isolated pockets left. Most of the weapons had been collected. They were stored in a heavily guarded warehouse. It would be safer to get them out of the city completely until the council decided whether to destroy them. He needed to bring up the issue at the next council meeting.

A few flakes of snow trickled down from a metallic sky. Winter was almost upon them. People needed fuel for the upcoming months. Nothing had been done about it yet.

Instead, Nield had recruited more and more workers on his mission to destroy every Hall in the city. Since Obi-Wan was on the streets most of the time, he had seen the anger of the people. They had turned from thoughts of war to thoughts of survival. The Young were not helping them rebuild their homes or feed their families. The unrest was growing. The Middle Generation had helped them win the war, but the Young were losing their support. What they lacked in numbers they made up in influence. The Young couldn't afford to alienate them.

We must do something, Obi-Wan thought.

He saw a group of Scavenger Young hurrying down a side street with a sense of purpose. Obi-Wan called to one of them.

"Joli! What's going on?"

A short, stocky boy turned. "Mawat called us. Another Hall of Evidence going down today. The one on Glory Street near the plaza." He hurried on after the others.

Obi-Wan felt a pang. That Hall of Evidence held the holograms and markers of Cerasi's ancestors. He remembered how wistful she'd been about her lack of family. Perhaps he should let her know what was about to happen.

He forgot his weariness as he hurried to the tunnels. He climbed down the grate near the mausoleum and hurried into the vaulted space. Cerasi sat at the scrubbed tomb the Young had used as a meeting table.

"I heard," she told Obi-Wan.

His steps slowed as he approached her. "We can ask Nield to stop —"

Cerasi brushed a strand of her short coppery hair out of her eyes. "That wouldn't be fair, Obi-Wan."

Obi-Wan sank down on a stool next to her. "When was the last time you went to the Hall?"

Cerasi sighed. "I can't remember. Before I came down into the tunnels. . . . Long enough so that I can't really remember my mother's face. Her memory is fading." She turned to Obi-Wan. "I believe that Nield is right. I hate the Halls of Evidence as much as he does. Or at least I did. But I don't hate my family, Obi-Wan. My mother, my aunts, my uncles, the cousins I've lost . . . they're all there. Their faces, their voices . . . I don't have any other way to remember them. And I'm not alone. So many on Melida/Daan have nothing to remember their loved ones by except the Halls of Evidence. We've bombed our homes and libraries and civic buildings . . . we have no records of births and marriages and deaths. If we destroy all the holograms, our history will be lost forever. Will we end up missing part of what we destroy?"

Cerasi's keen eyes searched his, but he had no answers for her.

"I'm not sure," he said slowly. "Maybe Nield

is being too rash. Maybe the holograms should be preserved somehow. Say in a vault that can only be accessed with permission. That way we wouldn't be encouraging the worship of war or violence, but scholars could have access, and we'd retain the history of Melida/Daan."

"That's a good idea, Obi-Wan," Cerasi said excitedly. "It's a compromise. And it's something to offer the people of Zehava."

"Why don't we persuade Nield to stop temporarily until we can figure this out?"

The excitement in Cerasi's eyes dimmed. "He won't," she said flatly.

"The council of advisors could issue a stop action on Nield's squad until further debate and study can be done. We have that power. Nield would have to go along."

Cerasi bit her lip. "I don't think I can do that. I can't oppose Nield officially. It would split the Young in two. We need to act together. If the Young is divided, that's the end of peace on Melida/Daan. I can't risk that."

"Cerasi, the city is falling apart," Obi-Wan said urgently. "The people want their lives back. *That's* the way peace will remain. If Nield concentrates on destruction instead of rebuilding, the people will revolt."

Cerasi dropped her head in her hands. "I don't know what to do!"

Mawat suddenly rushed into the chamber. "Hey, Obi-Wan!" he called. "We need you!"

Obi-Wan sprang to his feet. "What is it?"

"Wehutti has organized the Elders to protest the destruction of the Hall on Glory Street," Mawat said. "Yes, there's a huge crowd forming. I need you, now, to authorize the release of weapons to the Young. We must defend our right to demolish the Halls!"

Obi-Wan shook his head. "I'm not releasing any weapons, Mawat. That could turn a protest into a massacre."

Mawat pushed his hands through his long, sandy hair in frustration. "But we're unarmed, thanks to you!"

"Thanks to the unanimous decision of the council," Cerasi rapped out. "Obi-Wan is right."

Disgusted, Mawat turned away. "Hey, thanks for nothing."

"Wait, Mawat!" Obi-Wan called. "I said I wouldn't give you weapons. I didn't say I wouldn't give you help."

CHAPTER 8

The rumor spread through the Temple like wildfire. An intruder had been spotted on the grounds. Some said he or she had been seen in the Temple itself. The youngest students were afraid, and even the Jedi Knights were apprehensive. The Temple was on high-security alert. How could someone violate it? Was the Temple vulnerable?

"The Temple's security is tight," Qui-Gon told Tahl as they walked through the halls on a survey, TooJay ahead of them. "But perhaps it relies too much on closing down if a threat is out there."

"Meaning?" Tahl asked.

"Meaning, there are not as many systems operating to protect us if there is someone on the inside who *wants* the intruder to enter. The system assumes that no Jedi would welcome an outside threat."

"Ramp, incline fifteen degrees, two meters ahead," TooJay trilled.

Tahl's face tightened with annoyance for a moment, but she returned to Qui-Gon's statement. "We don't even know if there's an intruder at all," she said, frustrated. "We've tried to track the story to its source, and it's impossible. This one told that one, who heard it from this one, who doesn't remember who told him . . ."

"It's the nature of a rumor to be difficult to track," Qui-Gon offered. "Perhaps the intruder is counting on that. Perhaps he or she *wants* us to think an invasion has occurred."

A voice came over the address system. "Code fourteen, code fourteen," the calm, steady voice intoned.

"Yoda's signal," Tahl said. "Something's happened."

The two Jedi Knights reversed direction. This time, Tahl took Qui-Gon's arm so that they could move quickly.

"Master Tahl! Please slow down!" TooJay called in her musical voice. "I must assist!"

"Get lost!" Tahl yelled over her shoulder. "I'm in a hurry!"

"I cannot get lost, sir," TooJay replied, hurrying after them. "I'm a navigation droid."

Qui-Gon and Tahl hurried to the small conference room where they had agreed to meet Yoda for updates. The room was the most secure at the Temple, with a scanner that constantly monitored for surveillance devices.

Yoda was waiting as they entered the white chamber.

"Door to close in approximately two seconds," TooJay told Tahl.

"TooJay —" Tahl said impatiently.

"I shall wait outside, sir," TooJay answered.

The door hissed shut behind them. Yoda looked grave.

"Bad news, I have," he said. "Another theft to report. Stolen this time are the healing crystals of fire."

"The crystals?" Qui-Gon asked, stunned. "But they're under the highest security."

Tahl let out a breath. "Who knows?"

"The Council only," Yoda said. "But fear we do that word will get out."

Every time Qui-Gon thought the situation could not get worse, it did. The seriousness of the thefts was escalating. Which could be the point.

There is the pattern, Qui-Gon thought. *This isn't random. It's planned.*

This time, the thief had struck at the very heart of the Temple. The healing crystals of fire had been a Jedi treasure for thousands of years. They were held in a meditation chamber that was accessible to all students. The room's only heat and light source was from the crystals themselves. Embedded in the heart of each rock was an eternal flame.

When the students discovered them stolen, it would surely rock their belief in the Temple's invincibility. Maybe it would test their belief in the Force itself.

"Find who did this you must," Yoda told them. "But something more important you must find."

"What is that, Yoda?" Tahl asked.

"You must find *why*," Yoda said urgently. "Fear I do that in *why* the seed for our destruction lies."

Yoda walked out. The door hissed behind him.

"First step?" Tahl asked Qui-Gon.

"My quarters," Qui-Gon answered. "I have notes on my datapad. And from now on, we should carry our notes on us at all times. If the healing crystals are vulnerable, so are we."

Qui-Gon and Tahl entered the chamber. Qui-Gon had worried that his datapad would be missing, but it was right where he had left it, in a drawer by his sleep-couch. There were no locks or safes at the Temple.

"All right," he said. "Let's get back to —"

He stopped to watch Tahl. It was obvious his friend wasn't listening to him. She stood in the middle of the room, a look of intense concentration on her face. He waited, not wanting to interrupt.

"Do you smell it?" she asked. "Someone has been here, Qui-Gon. There is your scent in the room . . . and something else. An intruder."

Qui-Gon looked around the room. Nothing had been disturbed. He activated his datapad. All his coded notes were still there. Interviews with students, security procedures. Could someone have broken the code and read them? It didn't matter much. He hadn't recorded speculation, only facts. But still, someone had been here.

Sudden excitement rippled through Qui-Gon. Tahl turned, catching the change in his mood. More and more, it was extraordinary what she could pick up without seeing.

"What is it?" she asked.

"You just found a way to catch the thief," Qui-Gon replied.

CHAPTER 9

Obi-Wan, Cerasi, and Mawat emerged from the tunnel only a block from the Hall of Evidence. Obi-Wan had alerted all members of the Security Squad to meet him there. He did not want to use violence, but a show of weapons could come in handy. A showdown must be avoided at all costs.

But they were too late. A showdown was already in progress.

Wehutti and the Elders had formed a human chain around the Hall. They stood shoulder to shoulder facing Nield and his helpers.

Nield had apparently started the demolition before being outmaneuvered by the Elders. Some markers had been dragged out and partially demolished. Floaters packed with beam-drills and other demolition equipment were parked outside the human wall. Obviously,

Wehutti and the Elders had managed to get between Nield and the equipment.

Cerasi and Obi-Wan hurried over to Nield.

"Look at them," Nield said disgustedly. "Protecting their hate with their lives."

"This is a bad situation, Nield," Obi-Wan said.

"Thanks for the information," Nield said sarcastically. Then he sighed. "Look, I know it's bad. Why do you think I'm standing here, not doing anything? If we use force to break through them, it can backfire. But we can't let them win. We have to destroy the Hall."

"Why?" Cerasi asked.

Nield whipped his head around. "What do you mean? You know why."

"I thought I did," Cerasi said. "I've been having second thoughts, Nield. Is it wise to destroy the only place we have collected our history?"

"A history of death and destruction!"

"Yes," Cerasi admitted. "But it is our history."

Nield just stared at Cerasi. "I can't believe this," he muttered.

"Nield, we have to consider Zehava, too," Obi-Wan put in. "When I said this was a bad situation, I meant more than just the destruction of this Hall. If you insist on using force, the news will travel all over the city. The people are already unhappy with us. They're cold, and winter is coming. They need to see signs of rebuilding, not more destruction."

Nield looked from Cerasi to Obi-Wan in disbelief. "What happened to our ideals? Are we going to compromise so soon?"

"Is compromise so bad?" Cerasi asked. "Whole civilizations are built on it." She put her hand on Nield's arm. "Let Wehutti win this one, Nield."

He shook his head violently. "No. And since when do you care if your father is defeated? You didn't care during the war! You shot at enough Elders. You would have killed him if you could!"

Nield's words seemed to hit Cerasi in the face. She turned away.

"Nield, listen," Obi-Wan pleaded. "This isn't about Wehutti. We all want what's best for Zehava. These are matters we all need to discuss. We should put it to a vote. Isn't that why we set up the system of government? You yourself wanted the council. You didn't want complete authority, remember?"

Nield's dark eyes were stormy. "All right. I can't oppose both of you."

Cerasi looked at him pleadingly. "We aren't opposing you, Nield. We're still together." She held up her palm.

Nield ignored it. He turned away and stalked

off. He signaled to his squad, and after a moment, they followed, with baffled expressions on their faces. They had never seen Nield give up before.

The Elders let out a great cheer. Wehutti's strong voice boomed out.

"We have our victory!"

Cerasi's face was troubled as she watched her father. "I think I just made a mistake. I shouldn't have argued with Nield in front of them."

"I don't think we had a choice," Obi-Wan said, though he, too, was worried by the Elders' reaction. Knowing Wehutti, he would turn this into a great victory and use it to his advantage.

Wehutti suddenly turned and looked over the heads of the crowd, straight at Cerasi. Their gazes locked. Obi-Wan saw the bravado slip from Wehutti's gaze as he looked at his daughter. A softness took its place.

So he is a man, after all, Obi-Wan thought. For the first time, he thought there might be hope for Cerasi to reconnect to the father she longed for.

An Elder tugged at Wehutti's arm, and he brusquely turned away. Cerasi let out a small sigh.

"Nield said his parents were more than warriors to him," she said. "I feel that way, too. I know my father is filled with hate. But if I want to remember, I can recall love, too."

"I think love is there," Obi-Wan said.

"That is sacred to me," she said. "And that means that the memories in the Halls might be sacred, too." She turned to Obi-Wan. "Do you know what I mean? Is anything sacred to you?"

Unbidden, an image flashed in Obi-Wan's mind. He saw the Temple, rising through the blue skies and white buildings of Coruscant, impossibly high, flashing golden in the light. He saw long, cool halls, quiet rooms, rushing fountains, a lake greener than Cerasi's eyes. He felt the hush inside himself as he sat in front of the healing crystals of fire and gazed into their flickering depths.

The emotion swamped him. *He missed being a Jedi.*

He missed his sure, strong connection to the Force. He had lost that. It was almost as though he were a first-year student again, aware of something he could feel, but unable to control it. He missed the sense of purpose he felt at the Temple, the sense that he knew exactly where he was going and was content to follow his path.

And he missed Qui-Gon most of all.

That connection was over. Obi-Wan could return to the Temple. Yoda would welcome him, he knew. Whether he could be a Jedi again was up to the Council to decide. Others had left and come back.

But Qui-Gon would not take him back, nor would he welcome him. The Jedi Master was through with him. And, Obi-Wan knew, he had every right to be. Once broken, such profound trust cannot be regained.

Cerasi read the truth in his eyes. "You miss it."

"Yes."

She nodded, as though this confirmed something she'd been thinking about. "It's not a shameful thing, Obi-Wan. Maybe you were meant for a wider world than we can offer you here. Your destiny might be for a different life."

"But I love Melida/Daan," Obi-Wan said.

"That doesn't have to change. You could contact him, you know."

Obi-Wan did not have to ask who she meant.

"You chose as you had to at that moment," Cerasi continued. "From what you've told me of the Jedi, no one will blame you."

Obi-Wan looked over the plaza toward the gray sky, up into the atmosphere where a few stars were beginning to twinkle. Beyond them lay the other worlds of the galaxy, Coruscant among them. A distance of three days with a fast ship. Yet for Obi-Wan, unreachable.

"One will blame me," he replied. "Always."

CHAPTER 10

Tahl and Qui-Gon went through their lists. Every student, teacher, and Temple worker who had access to the various stolen items and could not account for their time during that period was cross-checked against the central list. They hoped to narrow down who they needed to interview.

The computer tallied the names. The list was narrowed to two hundred and sixty-seven.

Tahl groaned aloud when the computer read the number. "It will take days to interview so many."

"Then we'd better get started," Qui-Gon said.

One advantage they had was that the interviews could be short. They scheduled each one for five minutes only. All they needed was for Tahl to pick up the scent she'd smelled in Qui-Gon's quarters.

The short time between interviews meant

that students ran into each other outside the room. Gossip buzzed out in the halls. The rumors about the stolen crystals were starting. Soon, there was a continual pileup of students in the hall.

"Where is TooJay when I need her?" Tahl complained wearily at the end of a long day. "Somebody should take charge out there."

"We're almost through," Qui-Gon said. "Bant Eerin is next."

A gentle knock came on the door, and Qui-Gon activated the release. The door hissed open.

Bant was only eleven, and small for her age. A Calamarian, she thrived in moist, humid climates. Qui-Gon knew that she had been a special friend of Obi-Wan's. She looked nervous as she approached the table where Qui-Gon and Tahl were sitting. Too nervous?

Tahl didn't indicate any surprise or special alertness. But underneath the table, she reached out and grabbed Qui-Gon's knee.

She had smelled the intruder.

Qui-Gon looked at the slender girl again. Surely this couldn't be the thief! Bant's silver eyes slid away from his gaze involuntarily. Then she remembered her Jedi training and quickly met his gaze.

"You seem uncomfortable," Qui-Gon began neutrally. "This is not an inquisition."

Bant nodded uneasily.

"But you can see that with the thefts, we need to speak with all students."

Again, she nodded.

"Would you consent to have your room searched?"

"Of-of course," Bant replied.

"Have you ever violated Temple security?"

"No," Bant said, her voice wobbling a bit.

Tahl leaned over to murmur in Qui-Gon's ear. "She is afraid of you."

Yes, Qui-Gon could feel it, too. Why should Bant be afraid?

"Why are you afraid?" he asked sternly.

Bant swallowed. "B-because you are Qui-Gon Jinn. You took Obi-Wan away. All he wanted was to be your Padawan, but a short while later he left the Jedi. And I wonder . . ."

"What?" Qui-Gon asked.

"W-what you did to him," she whispered.

"The girl is innocent," Tahl said.

"I know," Qui-Gon replied heavily.

"She didn't know what she was saying," Tahl said. "Obi Wan's leaving was not your fault."

Qui-Gon didn't answer. The long day had taken its toll. He could march for hours, fight off ten armed enemies, and here he was exhausted after interviewing children.

Without speaking, they headed for the lake. TooJay had not shown up to bring Tahl back to her quarters. Qui-Gon was grateful not to have her trilling voice calling out every obstruction. If Tahl held his arm, she could move just as quickly as he, even over uneven ground.

They reached the lake, and Tahl slipped her arm out from his. She did not want to take any more help than she needed.

"We should decide on our next step," Qui-Gon said, staring out at the clear green lake, now dusky with evening shadows. The lake took up five levels of the Temple, and was land-scaped with trees and shrubs. Narrow paths wound through the greenery. One had the illusion of being on the planet's surface instead of suspended high above. "It's time to flush out the thief. We could —"

"Qui-Gon, I smell it." Tahl interrupted him excitedly.

Qui-Gon looked around. They were alone. "But there's no one here."

She reached down and trailed a hand in the water. "It wasn't a *person* I smelled. It was this." She held up her glistening hand. "I smelled the lake!"

Suddenly, the cloudiness of Qui-Gon's mind cleared, and facts clicked into place.

"We have to explore the bottom of that lake," he said.

Tahl's mind made the connection as quickly as Qui-Gon's did. "The thief is hiding the stolen items there?"

"Maybe."

"Obviously, I'm out," Tahl said ruefully. "How's your swimming, Qui-Gon?"

"Fine," Qui-Gon said. "But I know someone who can do the job better."

Bant's silver eyes widened as she opened her door and saw Qui-Gon and Tahl.

"I would never hurt the Temple —" she began tearfully.

"Bant, we need your help," Qui-Gon interrupted kindly.

Quickly, he told her what they needed. He didn't want to involve the regular Jedi security patrol if he didn't have to. Everyone at the Temple was still a suspect. But both Qui-Gon and Tahl were convinced of Bant's innocence.

The Calamarian girl was the perfect choice. She swam every day, and her clothes gave off a faint smell of water and humidity. That was the scent Tahl had picked up in Qui-Gon's quarters. Bant no doubt knew the lake bottom well. She could do the search more efficiently than Qui-Gon could.

Bant nodded her acceptance, her tears already drying.

"Of course I can do that," she said. "For a Calamarian, it's nothing."

Together, the three hurried back to the lake.

"You'll have to cover the whole lake," Qui-Gon told Bant as they came to the beach. "But I'm guessing that if something is hidden below, it will be fairly close to shore." He smiled at her. "Not everyone is as good a swimmer as you."

Bant stripped down to the suit she wore for bathing. "Don't worry if I'm underwater for a long time."

Qui-Gon was glad she'd given him the instruction after she disappeared under the surface. Even though he knew she was amphibious, the amount of time she could spend underwater still tried his nerves. He watched and Tahl listened just as intently for the small splash Bant made as she resurfaced. Each time, she shook her head, took a deep breath, and dived underwater again.

The illumination bank had powered down to dusk when Bant resurfaced again. Qui-Gon was ready to ask her to stop. He didn't want to exhaust the girl. But she waved at them excitedly.

"I found something!"

Qui-Gon slipped off his boots and waded into

the cool water. He swam out to Bant. Taking a deep breath, he followed her underwater.

The lake water was dark. He could barely make out the flicker of Bant's pale skin as they swam down, down to the bottom. Qui-Gon wished he'd been prepared. He should have brought an underwater glow rod and a breather. He'd been too impatient.

But suddenly the crate loomed in front of him, settled into the fine sand at the bottom of the lake. Qui-Gon circled around it. There was no plant life or algae on it, which meant it had only sunk recently.

He signaled to Bant to surface, but she remained underwater as he fastened a carbon rope around the container. He tugged at it, and the container rose. It was heavy. Bant grabbed part of the rope to help, and together, they pulled the crate to the surface.

Qui-Gon emerged, gasping for air. Bant was breathing easily. She treaded water while he regained his breath. Then they towed the container to shore. When he could stand, Qui-Gon carried it up to the beach.

He described the container to Tahl. "I've never seen anything like it before."

"I have," Bant said. She knelt and ran her fingers along it. "We have them back on my world. Since so much of it is underwater and prone to floods, we store things in watertight containers. Look." She found a hidden panel and opened it. "You can place things in this compartment. Then you close the panel and activate the vacuum pump. It removes the water, then slides the item into the dry interior compartment. That way you can put things in without taking the container out of the water."

"Clever," Qui-Gon said. "Can you open it?"

"I think so." Bant pressed another button. The hinged top popped open.

Qui-Gon looked inside. "The lightsabers!"

Qui-Gon searched through the items. "Most everything is here, but I think some things are missing."

"The crystals?" Tahl asked.

"Not here," Qui-Gon said. Disappointment thudded through him. But this was a start.

"What do we do now?" Tahl wondered.

Qui-Gon turned to Bant. "You have done well today. Can you keep what you did to yourself?"

Bant nodded. "I will tell no one, of course."

Qui-Gon ran his hands over the container. "I must ask you to do one last thing. Help me return this to where we found it." He looked at the calm, shadowy surface of the lake.

"At last it's time," he said. "We can set the trap."

CHAPTER 11

"I call for a vote on a stop action for the New History Squad's demolitions of the Halls of Evidence," Cerasi called out. Her voice echoed off the crumbling walls of the building.

For once, the council chamber was silent. All of the Young were stunned at the call to oppose Nield. Cerasi, Obi-Wan, and Nield were almost seen as one person by the group. The division between the friends was shocking.

Birds wheeled overhead in the blue sky. Occasionally, one would fly inside the open roof and perch above, and a shrill *caw* would split the air.

Deila stood. "I second the motion."

The room erupted in shouts and demands. Obi-Wan could only pick out some of them.

The Halls must be destroyed! Nield is right! Nield has taken this too far!

Cerasi is right! We need housing, not rubble!

Nield's face was still and white as he waited out the shouting. Cerasi gripped her hands together. As council head it was her job to control the crowd.

At last she stood and pounded on the table with the stone she used to maintain order. "Quiet!" she shouted. "Sit down and be quiet!"

Slowly, the boys and girls took their seats. Everyone looked at Cerasi expectantly.

She cleared her throat. "The council shall vote. On the issue of a stop action on the demolition of the Halls, vote yes for the action, and no to continue the demolition." Cerasi turned to Mawat. "You may begin."

"Hey, I agree with Nield," Mawat said. "The demolition must continue. I vote no on the stop action."

Cerasi turned to the next council member, and the next. By the time the vote got back to her, it stood at four against the stop action and four for it.

Cerasi gave a quick, nervous glance to Obi-Wan. There were only three votes left: Cerasi's, Nield's, and Obi-Wan's. Cerasi would vote for the stop action. Nield would vote against it.

Obi-Wan would be the one to break the tie.

"I vote yes," Cerasi said quietly.

Everyone looked at Nield. "And I vote no, for the continued peace and security of Melida/Daan!" he called in a ringing voice.

Now all eyes in the chamber turned to Obi-Wan. He heard the mocking *caw, caw* of the birds overhead and the moaning of the wind. His heart was heavy as he said, "I vote yes."

"The motion is carried," Cerasi said, swallowing hard. "The New History Squad shall temporarily cease all demolition of the Halls until further study."

For a moment, no one moved. Then Nield suddenly sprang to his feet. "I call for another vote!" he shouted. "I call for the removal of Obi-Wan from the council!"

Obi-Wan stiffened. "What?" Cerasi cried.

Nield turned to the crowd. "How can Obi-Wan get a vote when he is neither Melida nor Daan?"

"Obi-Wan is one of us!" Cerasi cried in shock.

"Nield is right!" Mawat stood, his eyes blazing.

"Vote again!" a supporter of Nield cried.

Obi-Wan felt as though he could not move. Never could he have imagined Nield making such a charge. He and Nield were like brothers. Just because they disagreed on this issue didn't mean that would change. At least not for him.

Cerasi took charge. "Council members have been elected for a one-year period. Nield cannot oust any of us just because a vote went against him. Obi-Wan was a hero of the war, and was voted in by an overwhelming majority." She banged her rock on the table. "The stop-action vote has carried. This meeting is over."

She stood and motioned for the other council members to do the same. But the crowd was angry. Shouts and cries filled the air. Someone in a back row pushed someone else, and a fight broke out.

"We must decide on our own destiny!" Nield was shouting. "Melida and Daan together!"

The shouting grew louder. Obi-Wan stood at his place, still unable to move. He didn't know what to do. Suddenly, he was an outsider.

He glanced at Cerasi. She stared out over the crowd, her face white, her hands gripping the edge of the table. She met his gaze with despair. The unity of the Young was disintegrating before their eyes.

In the days after the meeting Obi-Wan and Cerasi could only watch helplessly as the Young splintered apart. Nield would not talk to them. He moved aboveground and slept with Mawat and the Scavenger Young in the park. Heartbroken, Obi-Wan and Cerasi could only try to heal the division they had caused.

We cannot let this divide us, they pleaded.

But the divide only grew wider.

Nield worked on Mawat to convince the Scavenger Young to support him. If he had enough votes, he could overthrow the entire council and call for a new one. He targeted Obi-Wan as an outsider who had no right to make decisions for Melida/Daan.

"If he succeeds, war could break out again," Cerasi whispered to Obi-Wan late one night as they sat up together in the vault. "If the Elders see that we are divided, they will use the rift to divide us further."

"I should resign from the council," Obi-Wan declared. "It's the only way to end this."

Cerasi shook her head. "We fought because we believed in ending tribal rivalries. Remember our slogan, We Are Everyone? If we start singling out who hasn't been born here, how is that any different from tribal prejudice?"

"Still, it would heal us temporarily," Obi-Wan argued.

"Don't you see, Obi-Wan?" Cerasi asked despairingly. "It is already too late."

Obi-Wan got up restlessly and wrapped his cloak around himself. He drew comfort from Cerasi, but he needed answers she couldn't give. He said a quiet good night to her and headed aboveground.

The night was cold. He climbed onto a nearby roof in order to be closer to the stars. Reaching inside his tunic, he withdrew the river stone that Qui-Gon had given him as a thirteenth birthday present. As usual, the stone was warm. When he held it between his hands, it heated them. Obi-Wan closed his eyes. He could almost feel the presence of the Force. It had not deserted him. It could not. He had to remember that.

He needed Qui-Gon. His Master was not the most talkative companion, but Obi-Wan had not fully realized how much he relied on Qui-Gon's counsel. He could use it now.

Once, when he was Qui-Gon's Padawan, he had only to concentrate and he could summon Qui-Gon. Now he reached out and felt nothing.

Events were slipping out of his control. Everything he'd fought for was now in danger, and he had no idea how to fix anything. There were plenty of people to talk to on Melida/Daan, but no one whose mature insight he could depend on. Even Cerasi was at a loss.

If war threatened to break out, could he appeal to the Temple to send a Jedi as guardian of peace? Would they send Qui-Gon? Could he dare to ask such a thing?

And if he asked, would Qui-Gon come?

CHAPTER 12

Because of heightened security, the illumination bank was turned off. The darkness was absolute. Luck was with them, Qui-Gon thought. He crouched with Tahl in the trees by the shoreline of the lake. He could barely make out the glint of the water.

"At last we're even," Tahl murmured when Qui-Gon told her how dark it was.

They had calculated that another theft would happen that evening. They had seen the thefts fall into an escalating pattern. It was time to follow up on the stunning theft of the crystals with another crime. The thief would need to conceal what he or she stole, and would come to the lake.

Or so they hoped.

Tahl would not stay behind. He had argued with her and lost. If Qui-Gon saw who the culprit was, she could get the news back to Yoda.

Qui-Gon might need to follow the thief. Tahl had argued that they should not rely on com-links for communication. This was too impor-tant. And they needed to do everything as silently as possible. It was best not to tip off the thief.

"All right," he finally agreed. "Just leave TooJay in your quarters."

They had been waiting for five hours. Every so often they would stand and stretch each muscle in a Jedi exercise known as "stationary movement." That kept them awake and their muscles fluid.

The lakeside was so still that it was no more than a flickering of a leaf that alerted Qui-Gon to the presence of another. Tahl had heard it; per-haps she had even heard a disturbance earlier, for her head was already turned toward the sound.

Qui-Gon called on the Force to help him. He was dressed in a dark robe and blended in per-fectly with the vegetation. He kept himself per-fectly still.

A figure emerged onto the beach from their left, not from the path he had anticipated. The figure was hooded, but Qui-Gon saw that it was a boy. Judging by his height, it was one of the older boys. The stance was familiar, too. Qui-Gon did not have to wait until the hood fell back to reveal the gleam of a white ponytail to know that it was Bruck.

He leaned over and put his lips to Tahl's ear. He whispered Bruck's name, and she nodded.

Bruck sat on the shore and took off his boots and outer cloak. Then he tied a waterproof parcel around his neck, lit a glow rod and waded into the lake. He took a deep breath and disappeared.

"He's underwater," Qui-Gon said in a low tone to Tahl. "When he comes out, I'll follow him. You wait here. Don't move a muscle. He must not realize that he's being followed."

"All right," Tahl agreed. "If you're not back in fifteen minutes, I'll get help."

In minutes, Bruck resurfaced and swam with a strong stroke to shore. He walked out of the lake and pulled on his boots, then pulled the cloak around him. Instead of heading back to the turbolift, he chose an overgrown path. Qui-Gon knew it well. It led through the undergrowth toward the utility buildings that held floaters and hydrocrafts.

Qui-Gon followed behind. Bruck could be heading for a meeting. He could be heading to where he'd stashed the other stolen objects. Either way, they would learn something important tonight.

Bruck was being careful, but Qui-Gon was

more so. He had more practice in moving silently than the boy did. He followed Bruck by sound rather than sight.

The overhanging trees blocked out the surroundings as the path wound farther away from the lake. Soon they would be at the utility sheds. Would someone be there to meet Bruck? Qui-Gon picked up his pace slightly so that he could see the boy.

"Tree root, two centimeters ahead." A well-known voice split the silence. "Leaf frond, three centimeters straight ahead at eye level!"

TooJay! Qui-Gon stopped and went perfectly still. Bruck turned, his ponytail whipping around. He could not see Qui-Gon in the darkness. But he turned and ran.

It was no use following him. He would most likely double back and return to the turbolift. He knew someone was out here.

Disgusted, Qui-Gon turned back. Tahl was waiting on the path a few meters back. TooJay stood next to her.

"Qui-Gon Jinn approaching," TooJay said pleasantly.

Furiously, Tahl reached over and shut off TooJay's speaking mechanism. The droid waved its arms, but could not speak.

"Qui-Gon, I'm sorry," Tahl said rapidly. "I didn't realize that TooJay was looking for me.

As soon as I started down the path, she was behind me."

"Why did you follow me?" Qui-Gon asked irritably.

"Because someone was following *you*," Tahl explained. "They moved so quietly you might not have heard them. I was worried."

"Someone from the Temple?" Qui-Gon asked. "Could you tell?"

"I don't think so," Tahl said hesitantly. "Students and teachers, even workers, wear soft-soled boots. This person wore heavier boots. And the clothes had a whispery sound. Not like the sound of our cloaks or tunics. I think it's a man. The footfalls were heavy, and he brushed the icus leaves. He has to be close to your height."

"So there is an intruder," Qui-Gon said. "That was who Bruck was going to meet."

"Yes," Tahl agreed. "But not only that. He didn't hide in the bushes or try to track you through the trees. He knew the way. This intruder felt at home here. And he was not afraid."

A sudden chill ran through Qui-Gon. This was the scariest news of all.

CHAPTER 13

When Obi-Wan woke the next morning, he was alone. Most of the Young had already headed aboveground. Cerasi probably hadn't wanted to wake him. He was sure that she'd been awake when he'd slipped back into his sleeping area near dawn.

Cerasi had left him a plate of fruit and a muja muffin for breakfast. He ate, wondering when he'd get a chance to eat again. Each day was so busy. If he wasn't on duty with the Security Squad, he was trying, with Cerasi, to convince the Young that they needed to talk without anger.

Suddenly Roenni burst into the space. He hadn't seen much of the quiet girl lately. She kept to herself.

"Obi-Wan, they need you," she said breathlessly.

"Who needs me?" he asked, standing up.

"Everyone." Her eyes filled with tears.

"Roenni, start from the beginning."

"Nield has convinced Mawat that they must overthrow the vote of the council and demolish the Hall of Evidence on Glory Street," Roenni said. "He's gathered most of his squad and some of the Scavenger Young."

Obi-Wan sighed. He would have to deal with this.

"They have weapons," Roenni warned.

"Where did they get them?" Obi-Wan asked sharply.

"I don't know. But Wehutti is there with the Elders, and they have weapons, too."

Dismay filled Obi-Wan. This is what he and Cerasi had feared, what they'd tried to avoid. Open conflict was in the streets of Zehava once more.

He debated whether to try to find Cerasi. He could call her on the comlink. But he didn't have much time, and it was better that she find out about the conflict after it was over. He remembered how torn she'd been to see Wehutti and Nield at odds last time.

Instead, he sent the emergency signal to his squad, along with the location of the site. He hoped they would arrive soon so he wouldn't have to face Nield alone. The sight of Obi-Wan would not calm Nield. Still he had to try.

Grabbing his vibroblade, Obi-Wan headed aboveground.

When he got to Glory Street, his worst fears were realized. There was a large stone fountain with dry jets in the center of the plaza. Nield and his forces stood at the end of the plaza, holding transparent shields and carrying blasters and vibroblades. Wehutti and the Elders were opposite, all wearing plastoid armor and carrying weapons. They blocked the entrance to the Hall of Evidence. Only the fountain stood between them. It was an explosion waiting to happen.

Obi-Wan hurried toward them. "I order you in the name of the government of Melida/Daan to disarm!" he called as he ran. He saw members of his squad hurrying toward the spot, their weapons at the ready. He made a signal to them to stand fast. If they started shooting, the Elders and Nield's forces would as well.

"You do not represent the government of Melida/Daan!" Nield shouted.

Obi-Wan's squad gathered around him. They looked from Nield to Obi-Wan, and he saw confusion on their faces. Obviously, Nield had reached some of them when he'd called Obi-Wan an outsider. Even Deila looked uncertain.

Ignoring their hesitation, Obi-Wan quickly gave orders for half the squad to surround the perimeter. At least he could prevent this battle from spilling out into the city core. He had to prevent any reinforcements from arriving. This confrontation could not escalate into war.

He walked slowly toward the groups. He could feel the turbulence in the air, the hot emotion. He knew that everyone was just a hair away from using their weapons.

"Move aside, Wehutti," Nield said. "We won the war. Let us do our work."

"We will not allow the desecration of our ancestors by a band of brats!" Wehutti thundered.

"We will not allow murderers to be treated as the honored dead!" Nield shouted back. He raised his blaster rifle. "Now move!"

Suddenly, the grate in the dry fountain opened, and Cerasi swung herself up and out. She began to run toward the middle of the two groups. "No!" she shouted as she ran. "This cannot happen!"

"Cerasi!" With a cry, Obi-Wan sprang forward. At the same moment, shots rang out. In the confusion, Obi-Wan could not place where they came from.

But they hit their mark. Cerasi's eyes widened as the blaster fire ripped into her chest. Slowly, she sank to her knees. Obi-Wan reached her just as she fell backward, into his arms.

"Cerasi!" he cried.

Her green eyes were glazed.

"You'll be okay," he said frantically. "Can you hear me? You don't need luck. Cerasi!"

He held up his palm. She tried to raise her hand, but it fell back. Her eyes unfocused.

"No!" Obi-Wan screamed.

He felt for her pulse with shaking fingers. There was no beat of her blood, not even a flutter.

Agony ripped through him. He looked up at Nield and Wehutti. He couldn't form the words. It was as though he had forgotten how to speak.

Tears ran down his face as the pain grew and expanded to every corner of his brain, his heart. It seemed unbearable. His body could not hold this much pain. It would simply break apart. Yet he knew it was only the beginning.

CHAPTER 14

The shock waves of Cerasi's death echoed through Zehava. She had been the symbol of peace. Her death became a symbol, too.

But it was not a symbol of reconciliation. Each side took her death and fashioned it to fit their own ends. For the Elders, she was a symbol of the irresponsibility and recklessness of the Young. For the Young, her tragic death was a symbol of the inflexible hatred of the Elders. Each group blamed the other for her death.

The Young and the Elders were more bitterly divided than ever. Though Wehutti and Nield were both in seclusion, their factions patrolled the streets, now openly armed. Each faction gathered more support every day. The rumor was that war was inevitable.

Obi-Wan knew that Cerasi would hate what her death had become: a reason to fight. But he could not begin to struggle with meanings and symbols. He could only grieve.

Nield had not attended Cerasi's funeral. Her ashes were now being stored in the Hall of Evidence where her parents' remains were.

Obi-Wan was alone. The loss of Cerasi was with him constantly. As soon as he opened his eyes he felt it. It was as though his bones had left his body, leaving an empty, yawning space. He wandered through the city streets, wondering how people could continue to eat, shop, live, when Cerasi was gone.

He relived the moment over and over. He asked himself why he hadn't run faster, or started toward her earlier, or anticipated that she would be there. Why couldn't he have caught the blaster fire?

Then he would see the shock in her crystal eyes as the fire hit her, and he would want to scream and pound the walls. Rage kept him as occupied as grief.

The loss of her presence hit him afresh from moment to moment. The knowledge that he'd never talk to her again made him ache. He missed his friend. He would always miss her. She had been a vivid presence in his life. They still had so much left to say to each other.

So Obi-Wan kept on walking. He walked until

he was exhausted, until he could barely see. Then he slept for as long as he could. As soon as he awoke, he began to walk again.

Days passed. He did not know how to climb out of this grief. Then one day he found himself at the plaza where Glory Street ended and Cerasi had died. Someone had hung up a banner and stretched it between two trees.

AVENGE CERASI   CHOOSE WAR

Something snapped in Obi-Wan. He ran at the banner and jumped up to grab it. The material was hard to tear, but he kept at it, muscles aching, fingers stiff, until he had ripped it into tiny pieces.

Cerasi could not be used this way. He had to stop it. He had to take his grief and his love for her and fight to stop it.

He had to talk to Nield. No one else could help him.

Obi-Wan found him in the tunnels, in a room far away from the vault where they'd first met. It was a room they'd used for a short time as storage. Nield sat on a bench, his head down.

"Nield?" Obi-Wan entered the room hesitantly. "I've been searching for you."

Nield didn't look up. But neither did he ask Obi-Wan to leave.

"Our hearts are broken," Obi-Wan said. "I know that. I miss her. But if she could see what is happening, she would be furious. Do you know what I mean?"

Nield didn't answer.

"They're mobilizing for war and using Cerasi as a reason," Obi-Wan said. "We can't let that happen. It would violate everything she stood for. We couldn't protect Cerasi when she was alive. But we can protect her memory."

Nield's head still hung down. Was his grief so huge that he couldn't hear Obi-Wan? Or had he reached him?

Then Nield looked up. Obi-Wan took a step backward. Instead of the grief he expected to see, Nield's face was twisted with rage.

"How dare you come here," Nield said, his voice throbbing with fury. "How dare you say you couldn't protect her? Why not, Obi-Wan?"

Nield stood. In the small space, his head nearly touched the ceiling. His anger filled the chamber.

"I tried to get to her," Obi-Wan began. "I —"

"She shouldn't have been there at all!" Nield shouted. "You should have been watching her, protecting her, not rushing into situations trying to save strangers like a . . . Jedi!"

Spitting out the last word, Nield took a menacing step toward Obi-Wan. His dark eyes burned. Obi-Wan could see the unshed tears in them. Tears of grief and rage.

"Jedi, always with their minds on higher things," Nield continued bitterly. "Always better than those they protect, unable to connect with living beings, with flesh and blood and hearts . . ."

"No!" Obi-Wan cried. "That's not what Jedi are about! That's exactly opposite of who we are!"

"*We!*" Nield cried. "You see? You *are* a Jedi! You have no loyalty to us. You're a stranger. You influenced Cerasi, you made her oppose me —"

"No, Nield." Obi-Wan struggled to keep his voice calm and steady. "You know that's not true. No one could ever influence Cerasi or tell her what to do. She only wanted peace. That's why I'm here."

Nield's hands curled into fists. "Peace?" he hissed. "What is that? What is peace next to loss? Cerasi was killed by the Elders and they must suffer. I won't rest until every filthy Elder is dead. I will avenge her or die!"

Obi-Wan was taken aback. Nield sounded like a hologram in the Halls that he detested.

"What are you doing here, Obi-Wan Kenobi?" Nield asked, disgust choking his voice. "You aren't part of the Young. You never were. You're not Melida. You're not Daan. You're nobody, you're nowhere, and you are nothing to me." The anger left Nield's voice, and weariness seemed to pull him down on the bench. "Now get out of my sight . . . and get off my planet."

Obi-Wan backed out of the chamber. He walked through the tunnels until he saw a square of gray light overhead. He pulled himself up through a grate he had never been through before. He found himself on an unfamiliar street.

He was lost. He took a step in one direction, then another. His brain was reeling, and he couldn't gather his thoughts. They were clouded by Nield's words.

Where should he go? Every cord that connected him to his life had snapped. Everyone he cared about was gone.

Nield was right. Without the Jedi, without the Young, he had nobody. He *was* nobody. When nothing was left, where was there to turn?

The gray sky seemed to press down on him, grinding him into the pavement. He wanted to fall down and never rise again.

But as he reached the bottom of his despair, he heard a voice in his head.

Always here, you may come, when lost you are . . .

CHAPTER 15

Qui-Gon alerted security to be on the lookout for Bruck. They could comb the grounds more efficiently than he could. Then he raised the container from the water himself and dragged it back to shore. At least they could return the stolen property.

He retrieved Obi-Wan's lightsaber from the dry compartment. He hit the activator, and it shot to life immediately, glowing ice-blue in the darkness. It hadn't been damaged, he saw with relief. He deactivated it and hooked it into his belt next to his own.

Tahl led the silenced TooJay back to her quarters. She would coordinate the search efforts from there. Qui-Gon went straight to Bruck's chamber.

The boy wasn't there, of course. Security had already looked for him. It was clear that the boy had decided not to take chances. He was gone for good.

Qui-Gon looked around Bruck's room. If there was a clue here to why a promising boy would do such things, he couldn't see it. His clothes were neatly folded, his desk neat. What had been in the boy's heart? Qui-Gon touched the lightsaber on his belt. What was in *any* boy's heart? And why did Yoda think that Qui-Gon could see into them?

He had let the Temple down. Bruck's anger had been there. He hadn't seen it. Just as he hadn't seen the anger of his first Padawan, Xanatos. Or the unrest of Obi-Wan.

Wearily, Qui-Gon gazed out the window. The sun was rising. It was time to tell Yoda. One of their own had betrayed them.

His comlink flashed red — Yoda was calling him. He was most likely anxious for the report.

Qui-Gon took the turbolift to the conference room where he knew Yoda would be waiting. Yoda was alone in the room when he walked in.

"So you've heard," he said.

"Bruck our culprit is," Yoda said. "Troubling and sad, yes. Called you here for something else, I have. A message for you."

Startled, Qui-Gon looked at Yoda, but the

Master gave no clues. He activated a hologram instead.

The image of Obi-Wan suddenly appeared in the room.

Angrily, Qui-Gon turned away and started for the door.

"I don't have time —"

Obi-Wan's voice was soft. "Cerasi is dead."

The words hit Qui-Gon hard. He stopped and turned. Now he could see that his former Padawan's face was etched with misery.

"She was caught in a cross-fire between Elder and Young forces."

Sorrow flooded Qui-Gon. During his short time on Melida/Daan he had grown fond of the girl. He had understood why Obi-Wan had been drawn to her. This was a tragedy.

"Now each side blames the other for her death," Obi-Wan continued. "Even Nield is ready for battle. Wehutti's forces have rearmed. My squad has been disbanded. I have no command, no way to convince the others to disarm."

Qui-Gon took an unconscious step toward the hologram. Obi-Wan's face was etched with grief and something else, something Qui-Gon had seen on the faces of those most stunned by an awful fate: incomprehension.

His former Padawan stood in miniature,

hands dangling at his sides helplessly. "I don't know what to do," he confessed. "I am no longer a Jedi. Yet I know what a Jedi can do. And I know that only a Jedi can help. Qui-Gon, I realize I have done harm to us. But will you help me now?"

Qui-Gon's hand drifted to Obi-Wan's lightsaber, still tucked into his belt. He closed his fingers around the hilt. It seemed to hold some sort of charge, even though it was deactivated. Or was it the Force he felt, pulsing around him?

Obi-Wan's pale face shimmered before him, then disappeared. At that moment, he saw what Yoda and Tahl had been trying, in their different ways, to tell him. He had not been betrayed by a Jedi. He had been betrayed by a boy. A boy overtaken by passion and circumstance. The boy deserved his understanding. No, he had no secret way to see into a boy's heart.

Perhaps all he needed to do was listen.

"Send Obi-Wan a message," he told Yoda. "I am on my way."

CHAPTER 16

When Yoda told him via hologram that Qui-Gon was coming, Obi-Wan was overwhelmed. Relief coursed through him, and he felt the first surge of happiness since Cerasi's death.

But immediately, the happiness was replaced by worry. Qui-Gon was coming out of obligation. Would working with a silent, disapproving Qui-Gon be worse than working alone?

Melida/Daan is what's important, Obi-Wan told himself firmly. *I have to do what I can for the world Cerasi loved.*

It would take days for Qui-Gon to arrive. In the meantime, Obi-Wan had to wait. With time on his hands, there was nothing to do. Thanks to Nield's bitterness, he had been exiled from the Young. Perhaps there were some who disagreed with Nield's tactics, but if so they did not join with Obi-Wan. No one would cross Nield.

Obi-Wan felt as though he were a ghost. He

was not allowed to stay in the tunnels, so he slept where he could, or where he happened to find himself at night. Abandoned buildings, public squares, a park littered with the hulls of abandoned speeders. Life swirled around him, but he did not take part in it. Only his belief in Cerasi's cause kept him on the planet.

His only friend was Roenni. She often sought him out, bringing him food. She had given him a survival pack with a glow rod, and a medpac, and a warm, lightweight blanket for the cold nights. Obi-Wan was grateful to her for her loyalty, but concerned that if others saw them together, word would get back to Nield.

"He will be angry," he told her. They were sitting in a small park that had been the site of a battle in the last war. Grass struggled to grow amid the bare patches. Only one tree still flourished. The others were just stumps, their branches and trunks blown to bits.

Her warm brown eyes turned suddenly fierce. "I don't care. What he's doing is wrong. Nield is a good person. He'll realize it eventually. Until then, I'll protect you. The way you protected me."

"I don't know if Nield will ever come around," Obi-Wan said, remembering the hatred in his eyes.

"He's out of control because of his grief,"

Roenni said quietly. "Only you can save the peace, Obi-Wan."

"I can't do anything," Obi-Wan said, defeated. "I can't influence Nield. He won't even talk to me."

"Is that why you called for your Jedi?" Roenni asked. "Can he help Melida/Daan?"

Obi-Wan nodded and touched his river stone. "If anyone can help, it is Qui-Gon Jinn."

He believed in his Master absolutely, even if Qui-Gon didn't believe in him.

At last the day of Qui-Gon's arrival came. Obi-Wan had been instructed to meet him directly outside the gates of the city.

He felt a rush of pleasure as he saw Qui-Gon's tall, strong figure stride toward him. A smile of relief sprang to his face.

The smile slowly faded as he saw no answering expression. Of course there was no smile on his Master's face. His *former* Master's face. Obviously, the sight of his former Padawan filled the Jedi Knight with anguish.

Qui-Gon's expression smoothed and became neutral. He nodded at Obi-Wan.

No greeting. No inquiry into how he was. Fine. Obi-Wan could handle it. He had asked for help, not comfort. He nodded back his own greeting. The two began to walk together into the city.

Obi-Wan waited for Qui-Gon to speak. Why didn't he? If only they could talk about what had happened, if only Qui-Gon would give him a chance to explain.

He knew one thing now. He'd known it the instant he'd seen Qui-Gon. He wanted to be a Jedi again. Not only a Jedi, but the Padawan of Qui-Gon Jinn. He wanted everything he'd thrown away. He wanted his life back.

He didn't belong on Melida/Daan. He had been swept away by a cause. A just cause, a good cause, it was true. But there were other just causes in the galaxy, and he wanted to fight for those, too. It turned out that Cerasi was right. He wanted a wider life than the one he'd chosen on Melida/Daan.

He had found his true path again. That was good. Still, despair filled Obi-Wan. All he had to do was look at Qui-Gon to know that the Jedi would never take him back.

CHAPTER 17

Qui-Gon had expected the awkwardness. He hadn't expected the pain.

The sight of Obi-Wan's young, hopeful face caused him to feel angry all over again. Qui-Gon struggled against the feeling. He knew he was being harsh.

He couldn't speak. He didn't want Obi-Wan to hear anger in his voice. His first words needed to be calm.

So instead he merely nodded his greeting. He saw that his coolness had hurt the boy. And Obi-Wan had suffered so much hurt already. Slowly, as they walked, Qui-Gon's anger trickled away and compassion took its place.

"I was very grieved to hear your news about Cerasi," he said quietly. "I am truly sorry for your loss, Obi-Wan."

"Thank you," Obi-Wan said in a constricted voice.

"There are many things to talk about," Qui-Gon continued. "But I think such things would be a distraction right now. Any problems we have with each other mean nothing in the face of a planet close to war. We should focus on the problems here."

Obi-Wan cleared his throat. "I agree."

"What is the latest news on Nield and Wehutti?"

"Nield is massing his forces. He has the support of Mawat and the Scavenger Young now. He is trying to get the Middle Generation to be allies again. There is a rumor that a battle will start very soon at the site where Cerasi was killed. I know that Wehutti's followers are also arming themselves. Wehutti himself is in seclusion."

Qui-Gon nodded thoughtfully. "Is Wehutti directing his followers, or are they acting on their own?"

"I don't think Wehutti is even in contact with them," Obi-Wan said. "He'll see no one."

"He will see us," Qui-Gon said firmly.

Wehutti's door was locked and bolted. Qui-Gon knocked loudly. There was no answer.

"We know he doesn't want visitors," Qui-Gon said. He withdrew his lightsaber from his belt. "But I don't think we need an invitation."

Qui-Gon activated the lightsaber and used it to cut through the lock. He pushed open the door easily.

The hallway was empty, as were both rooms in the front of the house. Cautiously, they moved up the stairs. They checked one room after another until they found Wehutti in a small back bedroom.

Food trays littered the floor. Thick blankets hung over the windows, cutting out all light. Wehutti sat in a chair pulled up to a window, even though he could not see out of it. He did not turn as they walked into the room.

Qui-Gon walked into Wehutti's field of vision and crouched down in front of him.

"Wehutti, we need to speak with you," he said.

Slowly, Wehutti turned to Qui-Gon. "There was so much confusion. I was prepared to shoot, of course. But I don't think I did."

Qui-Gon glanced at Obi-Wan. Wehutti was reliving the day of Cerasi's death.

"There were more of the Young than we'd thought," Wehutti continued. "We didn't think we'd actually have to use our weapons. We didn't think they'd be armed. And I didn't think that my daughter, my Cerasi, would be there. She didn't carry a weapon, did you know that?"

"Yes," Qui-Gon said.

"I had seen her a short time before. She'd come to see me. You didn't know that."

"No, I didn't," Qui-Gon said gently.

"We talked. She wanted me to stop fighting the Young. I argued. It wasn't a good visit. But then . . . she suggested that we not talk about things as they are, but things as they were. Her childhood. We had a few good years, before the war began again. And I remembered it all suddenly. I hadn't thought about it in so long."

Tears began to fall down Wehutti's cheeks.

"I remembered her mother. I remembered my son. Cerasi was our youngest. She was afraid of the dark. I used to stay in the room until she fell asleep. I sat by her sleep-couch and kept one hand on it so she would know I was there. She would touch my hand from time to time as she fell asleep. I'd watch her," Wehutti whispered. "She was so beautiful."

Suddenly, he bent over in the chair, his forehead hitting his knees. Great sobs came from his body. "There was so much confusion," he said in a choked voice. "I didn't see her at first. I was looking at Nield. My wife is buried in that Hall. Her ashes lie there. I couldn't let them do it."

"Wehutti, it's all right," Qui-Gon said. "You did what you had to. So did Cerasi."

Wehutti raised his head. "So you say. So you all say," he repeated tonelessly.

"And now your supporters are mobilizing to fight another war," Qui-Gon said. "Only you can stop them. Can you do that, for Cerasi's sake?"

Wehutti turned to Qui-Gon. There was no expression in his eyes, and his face seemed bleached of all color. It glistened with the marks of his tears. "And how will that help Cerasi? I don't care about war or battles. I can't stop anything from happening, that's clear. I have no hatred anymore. I have nothing."

"But Cerasi would want you to help," Obi-Wan said.

Wehutti turned toward the window that had no view. "There was so much confusion," he said numbly. "I was ready to shoot. Perhaps I did. Perhaps I killed her. Perhaps I did not. I will never know."

CHAPTER 18

Obi-Wan felt a sense of hopelessness move through him as they left Wehutti's house. If Wehutti wouldn't interfere, war seemed inevitable.

Qui-Gon walked thoughtfully by his side. Obi-Wan had no idea what he was thinking. But that wasn't unusual. Even when they were Master and Padawan, Qui-Gon often kept his thoughts to himself.

They turned a corner and almost ran into Nield. Startled, Nield quickly skirted them. He did not look at Obi-Wan so much as look through him, as though he were invisible.

Obi-Wan's step faltered. He still wasn't used to the impact of Nield's hatred.

"You said that Nield accused you of being an outsider," Qui-Gon remarked. "Was this just because you opposed his decision to demolish the Halls?"

"That's when it started," Obi-Wan said. "He was angry at Cerasi, too. But things are worse now."

"Since Cerasi's death?"

Obi-Wan nodded. "He . . . he said that her death was my fault. That I should have been watching out for her instead of trying to save the Hall. He said that because of me, she rushed to the scene that day."

Qui-Gon looked at him thoughtfully. "And what do you think?"

"I don't know," Obi-Wan whispered.

"Nield has accused you of what he fears he himself did," Qui-Gon said. "If he hadn't been so adamant about the Halls, Cerasi would still be alive. He's also afraid that he killed Cerasi, just as Wehutti is. They are both afraid they fired the fatal shot."

Obi-Wan nodded. He didn't trust himself to speak. He couldn't think of that day without being swamped by feelings of guilt and loss.

Qui-Gon stopped. "Cerasi's death was not your fault, Obi-Wan. You cannot prevent what you cannot see coming. You can only do what you think is right at each moment as you live it. We can plan, hope, and dread the future. What we cannot do is know it."

You can only do what you think is right at each moment as you live it. Was Qui-Gon also talking about Obi-Wan's decision to stay? Hope rose in Obi-Wan. Had he forgiven him?

Qui-Gon began to walk again. "Here we have two grieving people who are secretly afraid they've killed the person they loved most in the world. Perhaps the key to peace is as simple as the answer to a question: Who killed Cerasi? Sometimes whole wars can turn on one tragic loss."

Qui-Gon had not been talking about Obi-Wan's decision. His mind was fixed on the problem at hand. As it should be. He was treating Obi-Wan with compassion, but it was compassion with distance. He hadn't forgiven Obi-Wan.

"But how can we discover who actually fired the shot?" he asked. "Wehutti is right. It was very confusing. Nield and Wehutti were both poised to shoot."

They stopped. Obi-Wan saw with surprise that Qui-Gon had brought him to the plaza where Cerasi was shot.

"Now, Obi-Wan. Tell me what you saw that day," Qui-Gon instructed.

"Nield and his forces were here," Obi-Wan said, pointing. "Wehutti, there. I stood here. Their weapons were raised and they were trading threats. Cerasi came up through the fountain grate. I saw her . . ."

Obi-Wan's throat closed. He cleared it and

went on. "I couldn't believe she was there. She began to run, and I ran, and I heard the blaster fire . . . I didn't know where it came from, so I kept on running. I was so afraid, but I couldn't move fast enough, and she fell down. It was so cold and gray. She was shivering —"

"Wait," Qui-Gon barked brusquely. "Stop telling me the story like a grieving friend." He softened his tone. "I know it is hard, Obi-Wan. But I can learn nothing if your emotions color what you say. You must remember without guilt and sorrow. Tell me as a Jedi would. Keep your feelings in your heart. Tell me what your mind saw. Now. Close your eyes."

Obi-Wan closed his eyes. It took him a few moments to compose himself. He searched for a clear space to let the memory come. He calmed his mind and slowed his breathing.

"I heard the scrape of the grate before I saw her. I was already turning to the left. She saw everything in one glance. She lifted herself out. As soon as her feet hit the ground, she started to run. She jumped over the wall of the foun-tain. I turned back to the right for just an instant. Nield was surprised. I saw Wehutti out of the corner of my eye. He . . ."

Obi-Wan stopped, shocked at the clarity of his memory. "He lowered his blaster," he said with surprise. "He didn't shoot Cerasi."

"Go on," Qui-Gon said.

"I ran, and I lost sight of Nield. I was facing Cerasi, trying to get to her. I saw the sunlight glint on the roof of the building across the square. I remember hoping the reflection wouldn't get in my eyes. I needed to see everything. I heard blaster fire. That's when she fell."

"Open your eyes, Obi-Wan. I have a question for you."

Obediently, Obi-Wan opened his eyes.

"Didn't you say that the day was gray? Overcast?"

Obi-Wan nodded.

"Then how could sunlight glint on a roof?"

Qui-Gon put his hands on Obi-Wan's shoulders and spun him around. "Look. Up there. Could you have seen someone *on* the roof? Could that glint you saw have been the fire from the barrel of a blaster rifle?"

"Yes," Obi-Wan said excitedly. "It could have been."

"And I have another question for you," Qui-Gon continued. "You say the Elders had weapons that day. But that was before they imported them from the countryside. Where did they get them? If you had confiscated all the weapons and kept them in your warehouse, how did the Elders manage to rearm?"

"I don't know," Obi-Wan said. "I assumed they smuggled them in from the country."

Qui-Gon gave a wintry smile. "You assumed? That does not sound like a Jedi."

Obi-Wan tried not to show how crestfallen he felt. Qui-Gon was right. He had been sunk in his own misery. He had lost the discipline of mind that was the goal of every Jedi.

Qui-Gon saw that. And now his former Master had even less confidence in him than before.

CHAPTER 19

To track how the Elders had been armed, Qui-Gon decided to start at the obvious place: the warehouse where the Security Squad had stored the confiscated weapons. Nield must have raided it. But could the Elders have stolen from it as well?

The walk to the warehouse was conducted in silence. There was so much silence between them now, Qui-Gon realized. And it was not the easy silence of companions. He saw the emotions that Obi-Wan struggled to hide. Chief among them was hope that Qui-Gon had forgiven him.

Of course Qui-Gon had forgiven him. He was not sure when it had happened — when he heard Obi-Wan's voice as he reported Cerasi's death, or when his former Padawan had greeted him at the gate with so much hope in his face. Perhaps it had been gradual, but it was there, in his heart, and he knew it.

Qui-Gon did not think of himself as a hard man. Obi-Wan had made an impulsive choice in the heat of a charged moment. It was a choice that he had come to regret. That was part of growing up.

Forgiveness was not the point. Qui-Gon had already passed to the next step. Would he take Obi-Wan back if he asked? He did not think so.

But that feeling could change, Qui-Gon told himself, struggling to be honest. It had before. So it was better to wait, to say nothing. Obi-Wan must deal with the consequences of his decision. One of them was uncertainty.

The warehouse was deserted, bolted on the outside with a strong lock. Qui-Gon sliced through it with his lightsaber and pushed open the door. A boy and a girl were sitting on the floor of the empty space, talking. They looked up, startled, when Qui-Gon strode in. He recognized the girl as Deila, one of the Young, but did not recognize the stout, round-faced boy.

Deila scrambled to her feet when she saw Obi-Wan. Then she appeared confused. Since Obi-Wan was no longer her leader, she seemed to be thinking, was it right to show him respect? Quickly, she sat down on the guard's chair. The boy made a halfhearted attempt to rise, but

Deila shot him a glance and he quickly sat down again.

Qui-Gon saw Obi-Wan's face flush. These two had once been his friends. But Nield had drawn a battle line, and they were loyal to him now. Qui-Gon wondered how far such loyalty extended. Why were the two sitting in an empty warehouse behind a barred door? They must have climbed in a window. Were they hiding?

"Hello, Deila," Qui-Gon said in friendly tone. "I'm glad to find you well."

Deila nodded coolly at Qui-Gon. "I am surprised to see you back on Melida/Daan."

"Certain factions on Melida/Daan have called for Jedi assistance," Qui-Gon answered. "I'm here to help."

Deila glanced at Obi-Wan. "I think I know which faction has called for help."

"There are many who still hope for peace," Obi-Wan said. "You were once among them."

Deila flushed. "Peace is always our ultimate objective. What do you want?"

"Just some answers," Qui-Gon said.

"I have none to give."

"I have not asked you a question yet."

"We're trying to find out how and when the Elders and the Young rearmed themselves," Obi-Wan said. "Did someone take the weapons? Obviously the warehouse has been emptied out." He turned to the boy. "Do you know, Joli?"

"Don't say anything, Joli," Deila said sharply. "We have nothing to say to an outsider."

Qui-Gon leaned closer and fixed Deila with his piercing blue gaze. He could use the Force on this girl, but it would be better to let her own emotions guide her. He sensed uneasiness in her. She respected Obi-Wan. He sensed that, too.

"You know that Obi-Wan fought hard for Melida/Daan," Qui-Gon said. "He shot down every deflection tower in Zehava for you, at great personal risk. He, Nield, and Cerasi devised the strategy that won the war. He fought side by side with you in that war. After peace came, he again risked his life to work for disarmament. If he is an outsider, he was also instrumental in saving your world. Now he continues to risk his life by remaining because he thinks he can help. Why do you show him no respect?"

Fierce Deila crumpled under Qui-Gon's gaze and became a mumbling girl. "I don't know."

"When you don't know your own mind, you fill it with the beliefs of another. Are you so sure that everything Nield says is true?"

Deila glanced at Joli. Perhaps Qui-Gon had

raised a question that they had been discussing. Joli nodded at her. "No," she muttered.

"Then will you answer my questions if you can? You can help the cause of peace on Melida/Daan."

Deila glanced at Obi-Wan. She bit her lip. "Of course I want to help the cause of peace."

Qui-Gon signaled to Obi-Wan.

"Where are the weapons?" Obi-Wan asked.

"Mawat took most of them," Deila said. "He moved them to a safer location, he said. I don't know where."

"Did he rearm Nield and the Young?" Obi-Wan asked.

Qui-Gon saw Deila's eyes slide to Joli before she nodded. "He heard that the Elders had arms, he said. Nield gave him permission. What could I do? Nield is governor."

So Mawat had just taken what he wanted. He'd known that Obi-Wan would refuse to open the warehouse. But how had the Elders gotten their weapons?

Joli's round face was red. He looked at Deila nervously. "I think we should tell them," he said.

"Be quiet, Joli!" Deila snapped.

"I don't want to fight in a war again!" Joli

cried. "You said you didn't either! That's why we're hiding here, remember?"

"What do you want to tell us, Joli?" Qui-Gon asked.

"Mawat armed the Elders that day," Joli burst out.

"Mawat?" Obi-Wan asked, shocked. "But why?"

"Because he *wanted* a confrontation," Qui-Gon guessed. "Isn't that right, Joli?"

Joli nodded. "If a battle broke out, Nield would be held responsible. Mawat wanted to make sure there would be trouble. He . . . he even put sharpshooters on the roof to start the battle if Nield or Wehutti backed down. He needed war."

"So that he could grab power," Qui-Gon suggested.

"He thinks Nield is weak," Joli said, slumping back against the wall. "Now he's planned another battle."

"Today?" Obi-Wan guessed. "Is that why you're hiding?"

Deila bit her lip. "He tried to recruit us. We hid instead. We don't want to fight. Especially since no one can find Nield. Mawat is planning a big action, but we're not sure what. He's acting on his own. He wanted me to set some explosives.

But he doesn't have the authority to start a war with the Elders!"

"I think both Mawat and Nield are crazy," Joli said. "We had peace on our world. Why can't we hold on to it?"

"That is a very good question, Joli," Qui-Gon said. "I wish every planet in the galaxy could answer it."

"So one of the sharpshooters killed Cerasi," Obi-Wan said as they reached the street. He felt dazed by what he'd learned. "Because of Mawat, she's dead. The funny thing is, Mawat loved Cerasi, too."

"The important thing is that Nield did not kill Cerasi," Qui-Gon said. "He needs to know that, and he needs to know of Mawat's betrayal. Do you know where Nield could be?"

"Any one of a dozen places," Obi-Wan said, thinking. "The tunnels. The park . . ."

"Let's split up," Qui-Gon said grimly. "We're running out of time."

He reached into his cloak and brought out Obi-Wan's lightsaber. He tossed it to Obi-Wan. "Here. I have a feeling you're going to need this."

Obi-Wan's hand curled over the hilt of the lightsaber. As he hefted it, the Force suddenly surged through him.

As he slung it into his belt, he lifted his chin and met Qui-Gon's gaze. For the first time since Qui-Gon's arrival, he felt no shame.

It didn't matter what Qui-Gon thought. He was still a Jedi.

CHAPTER 20

Obi-Wan went to Lake Weir, where Nield had spent happy times as a boy. He went to the Unified Congress Building. He went everywhere he could think of until suddenly he stopped dead and knew exactly where Nield was.

He was with Cerasi.

Obi-Wan rushed through the strangely deserted streets. Had the citizens of Zehava heard that a battle was forming? He didn't have time to worry about it.

Obi-Wan arrived at the Hall of Evidence. The entrance was pockmarked with blaster fire and beamdrill holes. He pushed open the door and stepped into darkness. He waited for his eyes to adjust, then walked down the aisle to where Cerasi's marker had been placed.

Nield lay on the floor, one arm curled around Cerasi's marker. A lump rose in Obi-Wan's throat. Any anger he'd felt vanished in an instant. He remembered Cerasi's tales of Nield's childhood. One person after another who loved him had been killed — father, mother, brothers, and a cousin who raised him afterward. He'd become a homeless orphan, afraid to trust or love anyone. Then he'd met Cerasi. If Obi-Wan's grief was terrible, Nield's must be even worse.

As soon as Nield saw Obi-Wan, he shot to his feet. "How dare you come here," he said shakily.

"I had to find you," Obi-Wan said. "I found out something that you need to know."

"You can't tell me anything I need to know," Nield shot back contemptuously.

"It wasn't you who killed Cerasi," Obi-Wan said quickly.

"You're right — it was you!" Nield cried.

"Nield," Obi-Wan said softly. "You know I miss her, too. We were friends once. What happened? Why do you hate me so much?"

"Because she's dead!" Nield screamed.

Suddenly, he rushed at Obi-Wan. He swung at him with his fists, raining blows on Obi-Wan's head and shoulders. Nield was wiry and strong, but Obi-Wan was larger and stronger, and better trained. It was easy for him to step around Nield, grab his arms and lock them behind his back. Nield tried to twist away.

"Don't struggle, and it won't hurt," Obi-Wan ordered, but Nield continued to try to free himself. "Listen to me, Nield. Mawat is the one who armed the Elders."

Nield stopped struggling.

"He wants a war," Obi-Wan went on. "If it starts, and if the Young don't win, you'll be blamed. I suspect he could be in league with the Elders. He wants to rule Melida/Daan, and he'll make any alliance he can to do it."

"Mawat wouldn't betray me," Nield said.

Obi-Wan ignored the protest. "Mawat wanted the shooting to start the day Cerasi died. He positioned sharpshooters on the roof. They were ordered to fire if you or Wehutti backed down. They *did* fire. That's how Cerasi was killed. It wasn't you. It wasn't Wehutti."

Obi-Wan let go of Nield's arms. Nield turned to face him.

"Mawat has been pressuring me to mobilize," Nield said reluctantly. "I went along at first. After Cerasi . . . I couldn't think. I could hardly breathe. But something happened to me here, next to Cerasi. I saw how wrong I was. How could I have wanted another war? Now I see why he was pushing me."

Obi-Wan heard sounds from outside the Hall. He exchanged a puzzled glance with Nield. There were no windows in the Hall, so they hurried to the front entrance. They peered out the beamdrill holes.

Mawat and a group of Scavenger Young were outside. They were busily placing something against the walls.

"They're wiring it with explosives," Obi-Wan guessed. "They're going to blow it up. That will provoke the Elders. And Mawat will blame it on you, Nield. Everyone will believe it. After all, you're the one who proposed the destruction of the Halls."

"We have to stop them," Nield said.

Obi-Wan noted Nield's unconscious use of "we." He withdrew his lightsaber and activated it. As it shot to life and he saw its pale blue glow, he felt encouragement rush through him.

"We can take them together," he said.

Nield nodded and reached for his vibroblade.

"Good luck," Obi-Wan said.

Slowly, Nield began to grin. "We don't need luck."

"Everybody needs luck."

"Not us."

Nield put his hand on Obi-Wan's shoulder. Their friendship had risen from ash and smoke. Danger lay outside, but they would face it together.

Weapons held high, they charged outside to meet Mawat.

CHAPTER 21

Qui-Gon hoped that Obi-Wan had more success in locating Nield than he did. The tunnels were deserted. Most of the Young had found quarters aboveground by this time.

He lingered in the vault where the Young had based their headquarters before the war. Perhaps there was a clue here that could lead him to Nield. He stood in the small adjoining room where Cerasi had slept with the youngest of the Young. No one had removed her personal effects, but someone had left flowers on her sleeping area with its neatly folded blanket and rolled-up mattress.

Qui-Gon smoothed the blanket with his hand. It seemed very poignant to him. Here Cerasi had tidied up on the last morning of her life.

He felt a small bulge in the blanket. He slipped his hand between the folds and discovered a holographic message disk.

Qui-Gon fitted the disk into his holographic message unit. Had Cerasi left one last message behind?

Obi-Wan and Nield threw themselves into the battle. They were outnumbered, but surprise was in their favor.

Their first objective was to prevent Mawat's crew from rigging any more explosive devices. Obi-Wan and Nield attacked furiously. The lightsaber felt so right in Obi-Wan's hand. He moved gracefully, his balance perfect, the lightsaber a blur of motion. Nield attacked with his vibroblade, slashing at the equipment boxes and rendering them into piles of scrap. The Scavenger Young dropped the rest of the timing devices and ran.

They beat back the Scavenger Young to a position on the plaza. There, Mawat had already organized the rest of his forces. Obi-Wan and Nield took cover behind the dry fountain. Its curving stone wall hid them from the blaster counterattack. But they would not be able to hold out for long.

"What are we going to do?" Nield asked Obi-Wan, ducking his head as blaster fire pinged into the stone, sending chips flying. "I don't have a blaster, just my vibroblade."

Obi-Wan quickly raised his head, then ducked

down again. "We're outnumbered, that's for sure. And Mawat has probably called for reinforcements."

"Well, at least they can't blow up the Hall," Nield said worriedly.

"We'll figure out something," Obi-Wan assured him. But inside, he wasn't so confident. He wished Qui-Gon would appear. Together, they could take on Mawat's forces. But with only one lightsaber, Obi-Wan didn't think he could protect Nield and fight at the same time.

Suddenly, blaster fire erupted behind them. Obi-Wan and Nield turned, startled. Deila, Joli, and Roenni were heading toward them, firing as they came.

"We thought you might need some help," Deila said as she landed next to them behind the fountain wall. "Roenni organized the others. They're going to come at Mawat's forces from the other side."

Just as Deila finished speaking, they saw more of the Young spill into the plaza, surrounding Mawat. At last the odds were even.

"Let's go!" Obi-Wan shouted.

They leaped up over the fountain wall and ran toward the battle. Blaster fire pinged around them, but Obi-Wan was able to deflect it with his lightsaber. With a sense of deep gratitude, he felt the Force enter and guide him. He moved without having to plan, anticipating where the fire would come.

Mawat whistled, and a squad of Scavenger Young suddenly materialized around a corner. They, too, joined the battle. Lightsaber swinging, Obi-Wan struggled to get to Mawat. If he could capture him, perhaps the battle would end.

A member of the Scavenger Young took aim at Nield with his blaster, and Obi-Wan swooped down, nearly connecting with the boy's wrist. The lightsaber seared his skin, and he let out a howl. He dropped to his knees, his face white with pain.

Nield and Obi-Wan exchanged a quick sorrowful glance. This was the ultimate wrong, the thing they thought could never happen. The Young were fighting each other. And they were doing it right on the spot where Cerasi had died.

As if they'd conjured her up, Cerasi's voice suddenly filled the air.

"I made my decision after the war ended," she said in a strong, clear voice. "I will no longer carry a weapon. I will fight no more in the name of peace. But today I might die for it."

Everyone froze. Obi-Wan felt his heart hammer against his chest. He looked around wildly. He saw Qui-Gon standing on the wall of the fountain. The Jedi held an amplifying device. The Young had used them in the early battles of the war, when they had fooled the Elders into thinking they had more weapons than they did.

Cerasi shimmered in hologram form in the well of the dry fountain. Obi-Wan heard the gasps around him. He looked at the faces, and he saw shock and sadness.

Cerasi had touched so many lives. She had pierced so many hearts. The Young had fought side by side with her, experienced loss and victory with her, had been inspired by her. Now, only she had the power to make them pause and listen.

"Do me a favor, friends. Don't build any monuments for me. Don't destroy any, either. History isn't in our favor, but that doesn't mean we should annihilate it. Don't let our dream of peace die. Work for it. Don't kill for it. We fought one war for peace. We always said that one war had to be enough."

Cerasi gave the cocky grin that Obi-Wan remembered so well. "Don't mourn too long for me. After all, I wanted peace." She shrugged. "Look at it this way. Now I have it forever."

Cerasi's image disappeared. The plaza was no longer filled with her vibrant presence. But an echo of her love and reason remained.

Beside Obi-Wan, Nield dropped his weapon. Obi-Wan deactivated his lightsaber. They both stared at Mawat. He stared back defiantly.

One by one, the others in the plaza dropped their weapons. They all turned to Mawat.

The defiance drained out of Mawat's face. He dropped his blaster.

The last battle of Zehava was over.

CHAPTER 22

Due to Qui-Gon's skillful negotiation and the power of Wehutti and Nield, a strong peace agreement was reached on Melida/Daan. Nield agreed to share power with the Melida and Daan Elders. No more would the city be divided, by either tribe or age.

Mawat returned to the countryside with a few of his followers. He had seen the city slipping out of Nield's control and saw himself as the savior of Melida/Daan. He had been wrong, and admitted it to Nield and the Young. Cerasi's words had reached him, too.

"Perhaps he can find his own forgiveness in the countryside," Nield said to Obi-Wan.

They stood in front of the fountain on the day of Obi-Wan's departure. He was planning to return to the Temple. He would ask the Council if he could return to the Jedi. Qui-Gon had agreed to accompany him.

Nield flung his arm around Obi-Wan's shoulders. "I gave you a hard time, my friend. It was good of you to find forgiveness in your heart."

"Sorrow can defeat the best of us," Obi-Wan said.

Nield gazed thoughtfully at the fountain. "I realize now how close I came to turning Melida/Daan back into the bloody battlefield I hated so much. The truth is, Obi-Wan, I was afraid."

Obi-Wan drew back to look at him. "You? Afraid?"

"I felt alone," Nield said simply. "I had a job that was too big for me to handle. I needed guidance, and there was no one to turn to. It seemed to me that every Elder and every member of the Middle Generation had no ideas. But I'm finding that's not true. I was listening to the loudest voices. Now I'm discovering there are others who share our vision of peace for Melida/Daan."

"You've created a new world," Obi-Wan told him.

"*We* did," Nield corrected. "Now I only have one regret."

"Cerasi is not here to see it," Obi-Wan finished gently.

*　　*　　*

Later, Obi-Wan trudged to the transport next to Qui-Gon. He longed to break the silence. Why was it so awkward now? Such silence was clogged with feelings, he supposed. Feelings that could not be shared.

He had to break it. He had to ask the question that tore at his heart. He was afraid of the answer, but it was worse not knowing.

"Will you ever take me back, Qui-Gon?"

The words hung in the cold air. Qui-Gon didn't answer, but kept on walking.

"I know I am meant to be a Jedi," Obi-Wan added. "I'll never doubt that again."

"I know you are meant to be a Jedi, too," Qui-Gon answered carefully. "But whether you are meant to be my Padawan again is not so clear."

Obi-Wan's heart fell. He knew it was useless to argue with Qui-Gon, or try to persuade him. Desolation filled him. It was not enough to be a Jedi. He had to be Qui-Gon's Padawan. Not because he'd failed him once, and his pride demanded a second chance. It wasn't pride that moved him. Deep in his heart, he felt it was right.

Yet Qui-Gon did not. Being a Jedi would have to be enough.

Suddenly, Qui-Gon's comlink signaled him.

He looked at the message. He paled, and his step faltered.

"What is it?" Obi-Wan asked.

"A message from the Temple," Qui-Gon said gravely. "A message of extreme distress. The Temple is under siege. An attempt has been made to kill Yoda!"

Discover how it all began.

JEDI APPRENTICE

Visit us at www.scholastic.com